The Unborn Odyssey: A Novel

Vajragoni

Copyright 2023 Vajragoni

All rights reserved. No part of this publication may be reproduced or transmitted in any form or by any means electronic or mechanical, including photocopy, recording, or any information storage and retrieval system, without permission in writing from both the copyright owner and the publisher.

ISBN: 979-8-9886629-2-1

Requests for permission to make copies of any part of this work should be emailed to:

vajragoni@unbornmind.com

This work is dedicated to my beloved and esteemed teacher, Tozen, who pointed the way and who began it all.

Preface

In a mesmerizing display of literary technique, this novel effortlessly unveils the profound teachings of Unborn Mind Zen in a manner that is both innovative and captivating. The author skillfully dissects the intricate principles of this ancient wisdom, rendering them accessible and comprehensible to even the most novice of minds.

The opening of the book immediately plunges the reader into the midst of the action, a literary technique known as "in medias res." This Latin phrase, which translates to "in the midst of things," is a common device used by authors to engage their readers from the very first sentence. By starting the story in the middle of a dramatic event, the author creates a sense of urgency and excitement that draws the reader in and keeps them engaged. This technique is often used in epic poems and novels, where the story is too complex to be told in a linear fashion. Instead, the author jumps right into the heart of the action, trusting that the reader will be able to follow along and piece together the backstory as the narrative unfolds.

As the pages turn, a new world unfolds before the reader's eyes, beckoning them to embark on a transformative journey of self-discovery. This unique approach weaves together the threads of spirituality, philosophy, and modes of consciousness, creating a tapestry of knowledge that is as enlightening as it is enthralling.

Through vivid storytelling and vivid imagery, the reader is transported to the very heart of Unborn Mind Zen. They witness the serene beauty of venerable masters imparting their timeless wisdom to the eager disciple. The air is thick with anticipation as the teachings are unveiled, each word carrying the weight of centuries of profound insight.

With each turn of the page, the reader delves deeper into the essence of Unborn Mind Zen. The prose effortlessly captures the essence of this ancient practice, guiding the reader through the labyrinthine corridors of their own consciousness. They are encouraged to question their preconceived notions, to challenge the limitations of their own minds, and to embrace the boundless potential that lies within.

The teachings, once shrouded in mystery, are now laid bare for all to behold. The meticulous breakdown of the principles ensures that even the most complex concepts are easily understood. Unborn Mind Zen becomes a tangible and practical philosophy and spirituality that can be applied to everyday life.

As the final pages are turned, a profound sense of clarity and enlightenment washes over the reader. They are left with a newfound understanding of themselves and the world around them. The Unborn Mind Zen teachings, once seemingly distant and intangible, now resonate within their very being, guiding them towards a life of peace, harmony, and self-realization.

This remarkable work has breathed new life into the ancient teachings of Unborn Mind Zen. Through masterful storytelling and insightful analysis, it has bridged the gap between the past and the present, ensuring that this timeless wisdom continues to inspire and transform generations to come.

The narrative unfolds with the profound teachings of Ch'an Master Tozen, the unparalleled Mystic of the Unborn Buddha Mind, intricately woven throughout the text. As the story progresses, the enigmatic figure of The Zennist also makes an appearance, adding a further dimension to the narrative.

Tozen's teachings are like a tapestry, intricately woven with threads of wisdom and compassion. He speaks of the Unborn Buddha Mind, a state of pure awareness that transcends the limitations of time and space. His words resonate deeply within the hearts of his disciples, igniting a flame of understanding that burns brightly within them.

The text also encompasses the further essential teachings of Unborn Mind Zen that also delves into additional profound insights, thus offering a comprehensive revelation that transcends the boundaries of conventional understanding.

Also included are essential teachings of Buddhism and Zen in general as well as the transformative teachings of Teresa of Avila and her Interior Castle. The renowned teachings of The Cloud of Unknowing is also included, which is conveyed through one of the characters—a woman veiled in mystery and awe.

The narrative also unfolds as a captivating blend of mystery and thriller, seamlessly weaving together influences from esteemed writers such as Colin Wilson and H.P. Lovecraft. A subtle nod to the enigmatic Franz Kafka adds an intriguing layer to the story, while the sacred mysteries of the Tarot lies at its very core.

In the midst of this enigmatic journey, a figure emerges from the shadows, shrouded in an aura of malevolence. Aleister Crowley, a name whispered in hushed tones, embodies the very essence of darkness and intrigue. His presence adds an air of danger and unpredictability, as his motives remain veiled in secrecy.

Within the depths of this enthralling tale, the reader is transported to a world where secrets lurk in every shadow, and the boundaries between reality and the supernatural blur. The text immerses us in a realm where the unknown beckons, and the human psyche is pushed to its limits.

Throughout the story, a recurring motif emerges, captivating the reader's imagination and leaving an indelible mark on their psyche. This motif takes the form of a towering structure, known simply as the Tower. Its significance extends far beyond its physical presence, for it embodies both the power of transformation and the essence of renewal. However, the Tower's influence is not limited to positive change alone, as it also serves as a catalyst for the destruction of antiquated ideologies and unhealthy ways of thinking.

As the story progresses, the Tower(s) stands tall and proud, their majestic silhouettes piercing the heavens. Their grandeur is awe-inspiring, captivating the hearts of all who lay their eyes upon it. It becomes a beacon of hope, a symbol of the potential for personal growth and metamorphosis. Those who dare to venture within its walls are forever changed, their lives forever altered by the profound experiences that await them.

Within the Tower's labyrinthine corridors, individuals are confronted with their deepest fears and insecurities. They are forced to confront the demons that have plagued their existence, to shed the shackles of their past and embrace the limitless possibilities of the future. Each step taken within the Tower's confines brings them closer to self-discovery, to a newfound understanding of their own potential.

As the story draws to a close, the Tower stands as a testament to the resilience of the human spirit. It serves as a reminder that through the trials and tribulations of life, we have the power to rise above our circumstances and emerge stronger, wiser, and more enlightened. The Tower's legacy lives on, etched into the annals of history, forever inspiring those who dare to dream and challenge the boundaries of their limitations.

Further on, the ancient wisdom of the Tarot also becomes a guiding force, revealing cryptic messages and hidden truths. Each turn of the page unravels a new layer of the narrative, leaving the reader spellbound and yearning for more.

As the narrative continues to reveal, the line between reality and illusion becomes increasingly blurred. The protagonists find themselves questioning their own sanity, as the boundaries of their perception are pushed to the brink. Shadows dance menacingly, and whispers of forgotten secrets echo through the corridors of their mind.

With each passing chapter, the reader is drawn deeper into the labyrinthine plot, unable to resist the allure of the unknown. The narrative takes on a life of its own, captivating and enthralling, as the protagonist's journey becomes intertwined with the very fabric of their existence.

Within the pages of this work, one embarks on a transformative journey, guided by the ancient wisdom of Unborn Mind Zen. As the reader delves deeper into its profound teachings, they are invited to explore the boundless depths of their own consciousness, unraveling the mysteries of existence and the true nature of reality.

The text serves as a beacon of light, illuminating the path towards self-realization and spiritual awakening. It unveils the timeless truths that lie dormant within each individual, waiting to be awakened and embraced. Through its pages, one discovers the inherent power of the Unborn Mind, a primordial force that lies beyond the limitations of time and space.

The teachings contained within this text are not limited to mere intellectual understanding; they are meant to be experienced and embodied. As the reader immerses themselves in the profound wisdom, they are encouraged to let go of preconceived notions and surrender to the vastness of the Unborn Mind. It is through this surrender that one can truly tap into the limitless potential that resides within.

The text also explores the interconnectedness of all things, revealing the intricate web of existence that binds us all. It emphasizes the importance of compassion and empathy, reminding us that we are all interconnected beings, sharing the same universal essence. Through this understanding, one is inspired to cultivate a deep sense of love and kindness towards all living beings, transcending the boundaries of ego and separation.

As the reader progresses through the text, they are drawn to the realization that all dualities are mere illusions. The Unborn Mind Zen teachings guide one towards the recognition that there is no separation between the self and the world, between the observer and the observed. In this profound realization, one discovers the inherent unity that underlies all of existence.

The text also delves into the practice of meditation and contemplation, offering practical guidance on how to still the mind and cultivate inner peace. Through the practice of Spirit Breathing one learns to quiet the incessant chatter of the mind and tap into the vast reservoir of wisdom that lies within. It is through this practice that one can directly experience the Unborn Mind, transcending the limitations of thought and language.

The book is divided into three parts, each section offers a unique perspective on different aspects of our existence, leaving no stone unturned.

Part one embarks on a journey of the Mind, inviting you to embark on an introspective adventure into the inner workings of your own inner-consciousness. Through a series of thought-provoking and insightful reflections, you will be encouraged to delve deep into the depths of your own psyche, unearthing the hidden truths that lie within. Prepare to be amazed as you unravel the mysteries of your own mind, gaining a newfound understanding of yourself and the world around you.

As you turn the pages to part two, you will find yourself embarking on a journey of the Soul. Here, you will be invited to explore the deeper meaning and purpose of your existence. Here, you will be guided to connect with your innermost self, peeling back the layers of your being to discover the true essence of who you are. This soul-searching expedition will leave you with a profound sense of clarity and a renewed sense of purpose, as you uncover the hidden treasures within your own soul.

Finally, in part three, the book seamlessly merges the insights and discoveries from both the Mind and Soul journeys, revealing the very essence of Spirit itself. It is here that you will be shown how to integrate these newfound understandings into your daily life, creating a more fulfilling and meaningful existence. Through a series of practical exercises, you will be equipped with the tools and knowledge to transform your life, bringing together the wisdom gained from your inner explorations and applying it to your external reality.

This book is not just a mere collection of words on paper; it is a powerful and transformative journey that will leave you with a deeper understanding of yourself and the world around you. Whether you are embarking on a quest to explore your own inner world or simply seeking a deeper connection with the cosmos, this book is an essential read for anyone on a journey of self-discovery.

So, my dear reader, prepare yourself for an extraordinary adventure that will challenge your perceptions, ignite your curiosity, and ultimately lead you to a place of profound self-awareness.

In conclusion, this text is a profound revelation that encompasses the teachings of Unborn Mind Zen and goes beyond, offering a transformative journey towards self-realization and spiritual awakening.

Part One

The Awakening

Evan's heart raced with anticipation as he lay flat on the cold, hard ground, his body pressed against the rough stone covering the cell. With his ear firmly against the crevice, he closed his eyes, shutting out the world around him. He focused all of his attention on the faint sounds that reached his ears, hoping to catch a glimpse of the elusive truth he sought.

As he listened intently, a strange sensation coursed through his veins, like a spark igniting a fire within him. It was as if a profound silence had descended upon everything, enveloping him in its ethereal embrace. In that moment, Evan knew that he had stumbled upon something extraordinary. "This must be the Luminous Light of the Unborn Buddha Mind," he thought, his heart swelling with awe and wonder.

With newfound energy coursing through his veins, Evan rose from his makeshift bed, his eyes still closed, his mind filled with the promise of enlightenment. And then, as if in response to his awakening, a beam of light pierced through the narrow crevice, illuminating the dimly lit cell. The walls and meager furnishings seemed to dissolve into the radiant floor, as if they were mere illusions, concealing the hidden depths beneath.

In the pure, radiant light, Evan's eyes beheld a figure draped in flowing white robes, a being so in tune with nature that he seemed to merge with it. Slowly, the figure revolved in the inner space, as if dancing to a celestial rhythm. It was a sight that filled Evan's heart with both reverence and curiosity.

Awakening from what seemed like a deep slumber, the Unborn Mind adept beckoned the Primordial, the ancient wisdom that resided within him, to guide him on his path. The Primordial, with his regal and noble presence, possessed a physique characterized by an aquiline structure. His gaze, like that of a poised eagle, exuded a sense of strength and determination. Yet, there was also a distant look in his eyes, as if he peered through a fog, glimpsing another realm, another time.

Evan, emboldened by his encounter, mustered the courage to approach the Primordial. With a voice filled with both eagerness and humility, he inquired, "I am desirous of experiencing the Way of the Unborn. What techniques ought I to employ?"

With a voice that carried the weight of eternity, the Primordial uttered words that echoed through the depths of Evan's soul, "Should you seek to pursue the Way, there is naught to be seized." These words hung in the air, pregnant with meaning and mystery, leaving Evan perplexed and eager for further understanding.

Not one to shy away from a challenge, Evan retorted, his voice tinged with a hint of frustration, "In the absence of any guidance, how shall I ever be able to execute what is necessary?" His words were filled with a genuine desire to comprehend the intricacies of the path he yearned to tread.

The Primordial, unperturbed by Evan's impatience, responded with a calm and knowing demeanor, "If you believe that you require some form of deserving guidance, you shall eventually realize that none exist." His words carried a profound truth that resonated deep within Evan's being, causing him to pause and reflect.

The Primordial continued, his voice carrying the weight of countless lifetimes, "There is nothing to seize, no entity to cling to, and no accomplishments to assert as your own. The essence of the matter lies within your inner Yin-Dragon, which will serve as your intermediary and maintain this connection.

"The Yin Dragon is said to be a representation of one's inner strength, wisdom, and tranquility. Legend has it that this mystical energy is born from the harmonious balance of Yin energy.

"When the inner Yin Dragon awakens, it emerges with grace and elegance, its scales shimmering in shades of midnight blue and silver. Its eyes, like pools of wisdom, radiate a serene and calming energy. With each beat of its wings, a gentle breeze of tranquility sweeps through the air, soothing the troubled hearts of those in its presence.

"It possesses immense power, yet it chooses to wield it with utmost restraint and wisdom. It is a symbol of inner strength, reminding individuals to embrace their vulnerabilities and find strength within them. The inner Yin Dragon teaches the importance of balance, urging individuals to find harmony between their light and dark sides.

"As the inner Yin Dragon soars through the vast expanse of one's soul, it brings forth a sense of clarity and understanding. It whispers ancient wisdom into the depths of one's consciousness, guiding them towards a path of enlightenment and self-actualization. It encourages adepts to embrace their sensitivity, and to find solace in the stillness of their minds.

"The inner Yin Dragon is a constant companion, a guardian of one's inner peace and serenity. It reminds adepts to seek solace in solitude, to find strength in silence, and to trust in the power of their own intuition. It is a symbol of resilience, reminding individuals that they possess the strength to overcome any obstacle that comes their way.

"In the realm of the inner Yin Dragon, time stands still, and the chaos of the outside world fades away. It is a sanctuary of tranquility, a place where one can find solace and rejuvenation. It is a reminder that amidst the chaos and turmoil of life, there is always a calm center within, waiting to be discovered.

"The inner Yin Dragon is a testament to the power of the human spirit, a reminder that within each adept lies a wellspring of strength and wisdom."

As the Primordial spoke these words, Evan felt a surge of energy coursing through his veins, as if the very essence of the universe had awakened within him.

In that moment, Evan understood that the path he sought was not one to be grasped or possessed, but rather a journey of surrender and trust. He realized that the answers he sought were not external, but resided within the depths of his own being.

Subsequently, the Primordial vision dissipated from his sight.

Believing that he had somehow understood the apex of the Unborn Odyssey, Evan proceeded to ascend the few steps beyond the door with haste. However, his stumble caused by the sudden obscuration of the moon by a cloud impeded his progress, and he then proceeded more carefully in the darkness. Upon reaching the grating, Evan exercised caution and tested it carefully, discovering it to be unlocked.

Nevertheless, he refrained from opening it, apprehensive of the great height he had reached within the spiritual vision. Then the moon emerged from behind the clouds.
The most alarming of all shocks is that which is characterized by the abysmally unexpected and grotesquely unbelievable. The terror he experienced from what he then witnessed surpassed anything he had previously encountered. The bizarre shapes that his sight implied were beyond comparison.

The sight itself was both simple and stupefying, as he beheld nothing less than the solid ground, adorned with marble slabs and columns, stretching around him on a level through the grating. The ancient stone church, whose ruined spire gleamed spectrally in the moonlight, overshadowed this scene.

Evan pondered, "What a pitiful and ruined spectacle. It is difficult to fathom that a once noble enterprise could meet such a dismal fate, now reduced to a crumpled heap under the veil of shaded moonbeams." However, Evan experienced a sudden surge of ecstasy upon realizing the truth. He concluded that the Primordial was correct in asserting that any attempt to seek external spiritual assistance was destined to fail. Such endeavors merely consist of vacuous structures that make hollow promises and propagate misguided teachings. Undoubtedly, the most effective method is to engage in the non-practice of the inner Yin breath, thereby ensuring maximum contentment and solace in the Unborn.

And so, Evan's journey continued, a tale of self-discovery and enlightenment, as he delved deeper into the mysteries of existence, guided by the whispers of the Primordial and the ever-present presence of his inner Yin-Dragon.

The Weapon of Choice

The encounter with the Primordial brought about a deep understanding and intense enlightenment. Yet, in that moment of deep introspection, as Evan fully immersed himself in contemplation, devoting all his mental faculties to exploring the depths within, something alarming took place. It is difficult to put into words, but it seemed as if, from the corners of his concentrated awareness, he detected the motion of an otherworldly presence. It was an unsettling jolt, similar to the sensation of feeling an unexpected, slithering movement against one's leg while resting serenely in bed. Initially, Evan had conceived that the presence of mind vermin could be traced back to antiquity. But here he was now experiencing the damn thing. Evan contemplated allowing it to pass, as he surmised that they were merely projections originating from the recesses of the dark psyche. However, as soon as he had commenced this action, the dreadful sensation commenced to escalate once more.

Suddenly, it occurred to him to initiate a state of non-action, in accordance with the principles of the wu-wei equation. For a period of time, this appeared to be the resolution; nevertheless, he was acutely cognizant of its continued presence, akin to a spider poised in the shadowy recesses of its web, ready to pounce. Adequate measures had been implemented. It was now imperative to solicit the aid of the most potent spiritual weaponry.

It was time to harness the protective capabilities of the illustrious Phurba. This Adamantine-Sword, also known as the Dhyani Buddha, Amoghasiddhi, is a symbol of unparalleled power. Amoghasiddhi, in his wrathful form of Vajrakilaya, utilizes the Phurba to counteract negative influences, particularly those of demonic origin. The Sanskrit term for this divine entity is 'kila' or 'kilaya'. The Phurba is adorned with the motif of a naga, with descending tails that converge into a sharp point at the triangular blade's end. Contrary to popular belief, the Phurba is not a mere inanimate piece of iron, but rather a mystical entity, brimming with vitality and energy. Any practitioner must approach it with the utmost respect and caution.

Traditionally, these "banning daggers" are crafted from iron, preferably from meteoric sources, to exert dominance over demonic forces. It is crucial to note that Buddhist practitioners who wield the Phurba do not seek to destroy, but rather to subdue and neutralize negative forces, much like isolating a computer virus. Evans Phurbas were crafted from a substance resembling marble, a testament to his refined taste and appreciation for the finer things in life. He wielded one at the moment, twirling it in his hands while chanting the sacred incantation to calm and subdue the hostile mental forces that persistently assailed him. The Phurba is a true embodiment of luxury and power, a divine entity that commands respect and admiration from all who encounter it.

OM BHASER KILI KILAYA SARVAR BING NE BAM HUM PHET

OM= A great sacred matter, as
SARVAR= any given polymorphous being is forewarned
HUM=and earnestly scolded
KILA, KILAYA=and forewarned with the phurba
PHET=the evil presence ought to disappear and release itself from any further evil intentions.

Evan held the belief that the origin of human power stems from a covert life force that dwells within the innermost depths of one's being. The utilization of the Phurba served to concentrate this understanding, harnessing energy like a focal beam from the Unborn Source Itself. This Source embodies the unchanging focal point of man's existence, his genuine essence, and is impervious to annihilation. As a result, the cognitive arthropods were rendered unable to gain entry to said Source. Their sole alternative was to surreptitiously siphon energy during its conveyance from the aforementioned profound Source to the conscious entity of sentient beings. The victory had been secured, at least for the time being.

Ascension from the Pit

Evan posited that the mind bears resemblance to a well-trodden path, akin to the grooves on an antiquated LP record that causes the needle to skip along its tracks. The navigation of these paths can prove arduous, particularly when the mind is fueled solely by the intellect. However, through unification with the Unborn, one can emancipate themselves from these grooves and truly delve into their Authentic Self. It is almost as if one can leave their [body] conscious self behind and explore the depths that the Unborn Mind exclusively offers. Evan once likened this to an iceberg, with only a small fraction visible above the watermark. However, he now realized that the conscious mind is merely a minute fraction of our essential beingness, and that there is an abundance of uncharted territory within ourselves to explore and discover. Within this realization there existed within him a glimmer of joy. The recognition of the void in all things elicits its own sense of elation.

"Indeed, quite a profound epiphany," someone exclaimed, as the recognition and resonance of the Primordial's voice reverberated within him.

"Yes, Evan replied; "however, it merely touches the surface of a more deeply profound matter."

The Primordial responded, "Recall the teachings of your former Ch'an Master from a distant past. Samsara represents a journey of the mind, an endeavor mostly focused on the physical aspect. It embodies a composed longing that arises from within oneself. This longing drives us to constantly escape one obstacle only to encounter another. The interconnectedness of these obstacles forms the essence of samsara, while the obstacles themselves are known as karma. Without understanding who or what exactly desires this perpetual journey, the obstacles will continue to deepen and darken. However, if we choose to change our ways and strive for a deeper understanding of our true nature, the obstacles will gradually become less significant. Eventually, our mind will rise above them, allowing us to observe samsara as a mere illusion, filled with fleeting shadows on a bright surface. It is in this profound reality that we can clearly differentiate between the superficial manifestations of the physical body and our own authentic selves. In that timeless moment, we begin to experience the first glimpses of nirvana, like heavenly droplets on our tongues."

In a moment that seemed to stretch into eternity, the Primordial, a being of immense power and wisdom, gently placed his hands upon Evan's head. As his fingers made contact with Evan's skin, a surge of energy coursed through his body, causing his brain to convulse with an intensity that defied comprehension.

In an instant, Evan's consciousness was transported to a realm far beyond the reaches of his imagination. It was as if he had been whisked away to distant galaxies, surrounded by a breathtaking display of a million points of light. The sheer brilliance of it all overwhelmed his senses, gradually desensitizing him to the dazzling spectacle unfolding before his eyes.

But just as quickly as the light had enveloped him, it began to fade, giving way to an abyss of darkness. The once vibrant points of light transformed into an endless expanse of nothingness, leaving Evan feeling disoriented and lost.

"What is the meaning behind all of this?" Evan pondered, his mind racing to make sense of the bewildering experience. It was as if he had been granted a glimpse into a reality beyond his comprehension, a reality where physical laws and boundaries held no sway.

As he grappled with these thoughts, a soft, inner voice seemed to echo within his mind. It suggested that the point of origin, the source of all existence, existed outside the confines of physical space. It was a concept that Evan struggled to grasp, for it challenged everything he had ever known.

With each passing moment, Evan felt himself slipping further into the depths of unconsciousness. The boundless emptiness of the abyss beckoned him, its alluring embrace promising a release from the constraints of his mortal existence.

As his consciousness faded, Evan surrendered himself to the void, his mind consumed by the mysteries of the universe. In that moment, he became one with the emptiness, a mere speck in the vast expanse of the cosmos.

"Have you had enough?" snapped the Primordial. Evan was gradually emerging from the tumultuous phantasmagoria that had been vividly presented in his mind. It was as though he was descending back into a realm of creaking wooden wheels, emitting an unprecedented agony.

"I am uncertain as to which is the more distressing: the burdensome weight of samsara or the haughty commotion of the ethereal realm."

"Both of these are the extremes of the enduring question of how to surpass them both. It is observed that, at their core, these apparent realities are exclusively creations of the mind, lacking in the attainment of Self-realization through the acquisition of Noble Wisdom."

"Is it safe to assume that Noble Wisdom holds a pivotal role?"

"Undoubtedly, it is the fundamental element for comprehending all enigmas of existence, which ultimately are not tangible but rather illusions of the perceptual consciousness."

"It is truly remarkable how the Lankavatarian adage rings true. It means that the way we think and reason has caused us to exist in three different ways. This has been happening for a very long time. But if we remember that we can be like a Buddha without any image or form, we can understand ourselves better. We can control our thoughts and actions easily, like a gem that shines in many colors. We can also change our form and understand the thoughts of others. By believing in the truth of Mind only, we can become a Buddha over time. It is truly a beautiful journey to witness."

Adaptation

Evan was deeply disturbed by the deplorable condition of humanity. Adaptation was key. The phenomenon of adaptation is characterized by discernible patterns. When confronted with a novel or modified milieu, an individual may either successfully adapt and persevere, or succumb to psychological distress and retreat from the challenge of confronting unfamiliar circumstances. Evan experienced disillusion, yet he was not deceived. He was cognizant that the panorama exhibited in front of him was a mere contrivance. It was simply a three-dimensional holographic projection, projected in space to simulate the impression of a palpable actuality.

Abruptly, an eerie stillness pervaded Evan's mind, a hush that he had never before fathomed. It descended like a shroud, rendering all noise impossible. The absence of sound and the enveloping darkness created an atmosphere of complete silence. His surroundings suddenly shifted. "Where am I?" he pondered. Initially, it appeared that he was situated on a flawlessly level and polished surface that extended limitlessly in all directions. This was an experience that his mind had never before encountered, vast and alien. However, it was soon revealed that the surface was not flat at all, but rather a dark and boundless tunnel that extended before him with spiraling lines leading downward and downward. He found himself spinning around and around, descending towards the vortex of the spiral. Involuntarily, he reached out to grasp something in order to halt his descent, but there was nothing to hold onto. Although there was substance present, matter and solidity, he felt different. His body did not feel right; a portion of it seemed to be absent, while another part was twisted and distorted, several feet away from him. Furthermore, his muscles were not functioning properly.

Initially, he experienced a sense of panic, but as time passed, the initial feeling of dread that had consumed him began to transform into a state of blind terror. It was as if he had been transported to an entirely different universe, one where everything was awry and nothing seemed familiar. This was a dreadful place that offered no solace or starting point, leaving him with nothing to cling to. As he attempted to block out this place from his mind and search for a way out, his terror only intensified. Even his physical body felt out of place in this environment, but his mind remained sharp and focused--one pointedness. Yes, biguan! This became his anchor, his only means of navigating this unfamiliar terrain. This was the only viable solution to his overwhelming sense of terror, and he was determined to use his mind to find a way out of this unsettling situation.

Evan's mind swiftly adjusted to the situation at hand, as if it were a well-oiled machine. As he stepped into this new realm, he could feel a distinct shift in the air, a sensation that was unlike anything he had ever experienced before. It was as if he had stumbled upon a peculiar dimension, one that was completely foreign to him. Yet, what made it even more intriguing was the fact that his own familiar world was just a few inches away, hidden around the bend.

What fascinated Evan the most was the realization that he had the ability to return to his own universe whenever he pleased. All he had to do was retrace his steps through that peculiar angle, now that he was aware of its existence. It was as if he had stumbled upon a secret passageway, a hidden door that led back to his own reality.

The entire encounter felt like a glimpse into a three-dimensional cross-section of a fourth dimension. It was as if Evan had unintentionally unlocked a portal, a gateway to the unknown. "So this is what it feels like to be in nowhereness," Evan mused to himself, trying to make sense of the inexplicable.

In order to find his way back to a more familiar environment, Evan cautiously proceeded to pass through that angle, almost as if he were opening a drawer in a desk. With each step, he could feel the energy around him shifting, as if the very fabric of reality was bending to accommodate his journey. And just like that, he successfully achieved his objective.

Suddenly, without warning, Evan found himself abruptly reappearing back into his own familiar domain. The transition was jarring, as if he had been transported instantaneously from one world to another. He stood there, taking a moment to catch his breath and process what had just happened.

As he looked around, everything seemed exactly as he had left it. The familiar sights and sounds of his own universe greeted him, reassuring him that he had indeed made it back. It was as if the portal had never existed, as if it were just a figment of his imagination.

Evan couldn't help but feel a sense of awe and wonder at the whole experience. He had ventured into the unknown, discovered a hidden realm, and returned unscathed. It was a testament to his curiosity and resilience, a reminder that there was so much more to the world than what met the eye.

With a newfound appreciation for the mysteries that lay beyond, Evan couldn't help but wonder what other secrets the universe held.

The Mind Mirror

The frigid gusts of wind that assailed Evan's countenance served to restore his equilibrium. He found himself enveloped in near-total obscurity. After a brief interval, the moon fleetingly emerged from behind a swarm of inky clouds, affording him the opportunity to re-orient himself. The ground beneath his feet was sodden and treacherous, indicative of a recent downpour. He proceeded with caution, mindful of the perilous footing. Clutching his metallic staff by its slender end, he employed it as a walking stick, and within a few minutes, he detected the unyielding surface of the pavement beneath his soles. The clouds once again parted, and the moon illuminated the thoroughfare that extended northward towards his objective.

The narrow, man-made canyons were shrouded in complete darkness, forcing him to walk with the caution of a blind man. He utilized the metal staff as a probing instrument and groped for railings or building walls with his other hand. The pavements were uneven and cracked, and at one street corner, he stumbled over the curbstone and lost his grip on the staff. The fear of losing the staff filled him with despair, and he struggled to control his rising panic. However, he remembered the mind mirror and activated it, experiencing a momentary pain in the back of his skull before feeling a sense of power and control. He located the staff with the guidance of a tingling sensation in his fingertips and a faint signal from the metal staff. Retrieving the staff from the gutter, he turned the mirror away from his chest, aware of the energy drain caused by such intense concentration.

The purpose of the Mind Mirror was not merely to provide an escape from reality, but rather to enable the mind to delve deep within itself, to reconnect with its original state. It possessed the ability to shift the mind's focus away from the distractions and disturbances of the external world, allowing it to recall its fundamental essence of being.

In this state of introspection, the mind found solace and tranquility. It was as if the Mind Mirror had the power to strip away the layers of external influences, revealing the core of one's being. It was a journey back in time, to a place where the mind existed prior to the burdens and worries of the world, a place where the essence of one's true self resided.

As the mind gazed into the depths of the Mind Mirror, it was as if a veil was lifted, and all other aspects of life became irrelevant. The mind became acutely aware of its own existence, detached from the trivialities and distractions that had once consumed it. It was a moment of pure clarity, where the mind could finally find respite from the constant noise and demands of the outside world.

The Mind Mirror was not a mere tool for escapism, but rather a means of restoration. It allowed the mind to recharge and rejuvenate, to rediscover its purpose and regain its strength. It was a sanctuary for the mind, a place where it could find solace and reconnect with its true self.

In a world where external occurrences held such sway over individuals, the Mind Mirror offered a glimmer of hope. It reminded people that amidst the chaos and noise, there was a way to find inner peace and reclaim their true essence. It was a reminder that the mind had the power to transcend the distractions of the world and reconnect with its original state of being.

And so, the Mind Mirror stood as a testament to the resilience of the human mind. It served as a reminder that, no matter how overwhelming the external world may become, there was always a way to restore one's fundamental essence and find solace within.

As Evan delved into his thoughts, he found himself reflecting on the distinct characteristics of the two cerebral hemispheres that reside within our cognitive abilities. It became clear to him that the left hemisphere tends to direct its attention outward, towards the external world, while the right hemisphere is more focused on our inner selves. The left hemisphere is primarily concerned with managing the challenges of everyday life, while the right hemisphere takes charge of our emotional states, sentiments, and energy levels.

In moments of tension and exhaustion, Evan realized that the solution lies in immersing oneself in a task that replenishes deep energy reserves. It seemed that the prevailing principle suggests that when one needs assistance and support, it is necessary to turn to the "other self" residing in the right hemisphere of the brain. This phenomenon reminded Evan of Wordsworth's "Intimations of Immortality" Ode.

In this poem, the poet experiences despondency and weariness, feeling pessimistic about his diminishing ability to find poetic inspiration. However, as he articulates these sentiments into language, he begins to realize that his situation is not as dire as he initially thought. With newfound assurance, he composes verses that speak of a resurgent sense of fortitude and hopefulness. This process exemplifies how expressing one's emotions can lead to a shift in perspective and a renewed sense of purpose.

Evan also observed that individuals who have suffered significant personal loss often turn to religious faith as a substitute. Their anguish compels them to introspect, and in response, the right hemisphere of the brain offers solace and motivation. The left-brain self becomes aware that it is not alone and believes it has encountered God. While this may indeed be the case, it has also discovered its "silent partner" residing just a few centimeters away – the Unborn Mind. This realization, in itself, is a profound revelation.

In conclusion, Evan contemplated the inherent characteristics of the two cerebral hemispheres and their roles in our cognitive faculties. He recognized the importance of turning inward for support and replenishment, as well as the power of expressing emotions and finding solace in faith. The collaboration between the left and right hemispheres of the brain, and the discovery of the Unborn Mind as a silent partner, revealed the complexity and interconnectedness of our inner selves.

Evan proceeded to circumambulate before an immense Tower before him, intently scrutinizing its exterior in an attempt to discern any indication of an ingress. Regrettably, the impeccably polished alabaster surface exhibited no discernible crevice or aperture. Despite this, he persisted in experiencing a peculiar, prickling sensation, accompanied by a pungent, metallic aroma. He was resolute in his endeavor to uncover the clandestine entrance of the edifice towering before him...

The Resurgence of the Venerable Teacher

This impression endured for a fleeting moment, until his eyes readjusted and he was abruptly transported to the shoreline of an expansive beach, which appeared to be of an otherworldly magnitude, with colossal worlds suspended in the distance. Initially, he was under the impression that he was in a state of reverie. However, the authenticity of the waves crashing a few yards away from him and the slimy, algae-covered rocks that extended into the ocean could not be disputed. He ventured forth to discover what this new reality might bring.

Upon scanning the beach for a second time, he spotted an elderly gentleman perched atop a boulder. The sight jolted him, as he was certain the shoreline had been vacant just moments prior. However, he harbored no uncertainty that he was in the presence of a venerable entity. As he drew nearer to the aged figure, he was overcome with a profound sense of admiration and respect.

Upon the old man lifting his head, Evan was struck with yet another surprise as he recognized his former Ch'an Master.

"What is the significance of all this? Where has the Tower disappeared to? How is it that you are present here?"

The old man began to speak, his voice carrying a weight of wisdom that resonated deep within Evan's soul. He explained that the beach they now found themselves on was not a physical place, but rather a manifestation of their consciousness. It was a realm where the boundaries of reality were blurred, and the possibilities were endless.

"The Tower," the Ch'an Master said, his eyes twinkling with ancient knowledge, "has not disappeared. It exists within you, as it always has. This beach is a reflection of your inner world, a canvas upon which your thoughts and desires are projected."

Evan listened intently, his mind racing to comprehend the profound implications of what he was being told. The Ch'an Master continued, his voice soothing and melodic, guiding Evan through the depths of his own consciousness.

"You see, my dear student, the world we perceive is not fixed or absolute. It is shaped by our thoughts, beliefs, and experiences. This beach, this otherworldly expanse, is a reminder that reality is malleable, that we have the power to create and shape our own existence."

As the Ch'an Master spoke, Evan's perception of the beach began to shift. The colossal worlds that had once hung in the distance now seemed closer, more tangible. The crashing waves took on a rhythm that echoed the beating of his own heart. The slimy rocks transformed into stepping stones, inviting him to explore the depths of this new reality.

With newfound clarity, Evan turned to his former Master, gratitude and curiosity shining in his eyes. "What do I do now? How do I navigate this realm of infinite possibilities?"

The Ch'an Master smiled, his eyes filled with a profound understanding. "You must learn to trust yourself, to listen to the whispers of your own intuition. Embrace the unknown, for it is in the exploration of the unfamiliar that we truly discover who we are."

"Can you explain more?"

"In essence, it signifies the antithetical actuality that precedes the unenlightened and impulsive ideation of the mind. The said ideation is predominantly founded on a responsive and immediately comprehensible amalgamation of phenomena. This, naturally, stems from the Mind's customary abode in an image-matrix that it perceives as a corporeal entity, through which it "transmutes" or alters the magnificent intelligible radiance of the Buddhas into something that it deems to be veritable reality, but in actuality, is erroneous.

"As our illustrious Buddha family expounds upon the awe-inspiring intuitive Light of this word, it radiates outwards in all ten directions, birthing countless universes and infinite worlds, such as the opulent imagery that dances before your very consciousness. Every conceivable image is brought to life and set into motion, creating a tapestry of unparalleled beauty and wonder. These myriad matrixes, each one perfect in its form and exquisitely empty, are made available to those who suffer, those who are ignorant, and those who slumber in darkness. Such boundless compassion is extended to those who have yet to awaken to the enlightened mind of the bodhisattva.

"As a Lankavatarian, one who follows the precepts of the Lankavatara Sutra, it is imperative that you comprehend that our perception of the world is one of a tangible and cerebral amalgamation. Every facet of our surroundings is imbued with a profound intelligibility, without which our very capacity for thought would be rendered null and void.

Alas, for the sensualist, their perception is limited to the superficial, the mere semblance of things. They fail to delve deeper, to uncover the intricate intellectual orders that underlie the raw appearance of our world. From the ethereal concept of space to the relentless force of gravity, every aspect of our reality is governed by a complex interplay of motion, energy, and time."

"How best to dissolve this imagery?"

"The discerning Mind must come to realize that through its awe-inspiring power to intellectually synthesize the emergence of its own cherished, yet fleeting, corporeal genetic framework [body], it can also gradually dismantle this illusory image and all "surrounding" images [perceived through the senses of this physical abode] by resolutely abiding in its authentic self, which is Unborn, uncreated, unconditioned, and thus the "word" itself. It was born out of a failure to grasp the potency of this word, and it shall likewise perish, writhing in agony, due to its inability to comprehend the transformative might of this word."

"So what will be my greatest discovery?"

"Discovering the womb of engulfing light is the first step towards unveiling the true boundless self that lies within. It is a self that transcends the mortal carcass and all that is experienced through the six senses. In this samadhic bliss, you give birth to your bodhi-child, also known as bodhicitta, but few understand the truth about its nature.

"This child is the seed that will awaken and recollect its true nature, the Buddha Mind, just as Siddharta did. Therefore, it is of utmost importance that you do not waste your time on a useless zafu with a blank mind, counting and following breaths, or engaging in other futile activities.

"Instead, have faith in the power of words and let your mind abide firmly like Bodhidharmas "inner" wall in accordance with their meaning. By upholding this in all that you do, you will be assured a straight and directive path to the deathless family of the Buddha's.

"Life, death, and all phenomena will no longer hold any meaning worth suffering for. Soon, your true teachers will appear and expound the marvelous dharma. You will witness the awesome compassionate wisdom of Avalokitesvara, Manjusri's uncompromising way to slay the false and reveal the true, and much more. Embrace this luxury of enlightenment and let it guide you towards the ultimate truth."

The Lower and the Higher

"What is the enigma shrouding the Tower?" inquired Evan

The teacher replied, "My sole objective is to consistently assist you in unraveling the most significant enigma of all. This mystery surpasses all others, both past and future. Once you have deciphered it, all other mysteries will gradually become apparent, as they are illuminated by this one."

"May I inquire as to the nature of this enigma?"

"It is none other than the authentic essence of the Unborn Mind."

"The direct-pointer to Self-realization, yes?"

"Indeed, the sole means of Self-realization is to extend an invitation to and relinquish the Mind to the elevated aspect of Bodhi. In due course, this aspect will manifest as an undeniable reality, prompting the individual to awaken and revel in a state of blissful comprehension, exclaiming, 'Now I finally know.' This realization will serve to fortify the individual's resolve towards their bodhisattvic journey towards Universal enlightenment, or the very cradle of the Unborn Mind."

"Pardon me, but could you clarify who the sleeper refers to? Additionally, could you expound upon the concept of the higher aspect of Bodhi? Is there a corresponding lower aspect?"

"Indeed, Bodhi possesses two distinct aspects, namely a higher and a lower aspect. The lower aspect pertains to the animating force that is currently being utilized by yourself to perpetuate this world and your own existence within it. This aspect is subject to your skandha-based will and merit, and as such, you have the power to determine your own destiny and the experiences that you encounter and learn from. This lower aspect is also referred to as the Bodhipower of your 'sleeping Buddha', which has the potential to awaken when it is reunited with the higher aspect. Contrary to the teachings of Dogen, it is important to note that you are not inherently a Buddha, nor do you possess a Buddha Mind from birth. Rather, as a sentient being, you possess the potential to awaken the 'sleeping Buddha', which is currently dreaming your existence."

"Could you please provide further elaboration on the matter at hand?"

"Certainly. You are, in essence, a mere figment of imagination in the dormant potential of a Buddha. Despite the peculiarity of this statement, a thorough analysis of the true meaning of a sentient being will lead to the realization of its inherent nature and the necessity to cease the cycle of perpetual 'becoming'. This cessation will awaken the dormant Buddha and ultimately lead to liberation from any illusory suffering caused by imagined dukkha.

"As one delves deeper into the realm of Bodhi, one discovers the exquisite essence of countless Buddhas, fully awakened and ceaselessly emanating Bodhi in all ten directions, illuminating the path for those who slumber. It is important to note that a Buddha is also known as a Light-bringer or 'light-maker'. The higher aspect of Bodhi is revealed through their will and Noble Wisdom, not through one's own. Its power is beyond measure, far surpassing the limits of human imagination. To embrace its reality, known as Tathata, one must transcend the skandha matrix and awaken to its presence, entering the dark principle of the Unborn Mind. This surrender invites a most mystical Initiation, a <union> between the Lower and the Higher, a divine merging of the self with the infinite.

"At a certain point, the perfect conditions align for the initiation into the spiritual community of the Buddhas. The one who is on a lower level of understanding is now prepared to catch a glimpse of the higher realm. As a result, the initiation occurs according to the <will> of the higher power, rather than one's own desires. This concept is also depicted in the Christian Bible when Jesus speaks these words, revealing that he wishes for the suffering to be relieved, but ultimately submits to the greater divine plan: "Father, if you are willing, please take this suffering away from me. Yet, I defer to your will and your plan" (Luke 22:42)

"If the appropriate conditions are met, one may experience a powerful energy or "wind" that permeates their being or mind. This sensation may be accompanied by a remarkable sense of elevation or ascension, which can also be perceived as an infinite expansion. Therefore, it is imperative that one's mind is trained to remain in a constant state of 4th Dhyana, a stage that is distant from the majority of individuals who are preoccupied with phenomena and meaningless pursuits.

"There are ample individuals who waste their time engaging in fruitless activities, such as sitting idly, and mistakenly believe that such practices will lead to liberation. However, I must emphasize that even if they were to sit for countless kalpas, they would only experience lower spiritual states that hold no value, and they would not be able to progress to the second or third dhyana level. Instead, they would likely become ensnared in one or more of the 50 false enlightenments mentioned in the Shurangama Sutra, perpetuating their imagined dissatisfaction."

"May I ask if sitting is incorrect then?"

"No, it is not incorrect. However, the Mind must detach itself from the concepts of sitting, walking, breathing, and other similar notions. It should instead concentrate on transcending these illusory phenomena and seek fulfillment within itself. Those who focus on following the infinite self-induced phenomena of the Mind, believing that this posterior and unwholesome act can lead to enlightenment, are so foolish that a new term must be coined to classify this degree of stupidity."

"OK then, I agree wholeheartedly."

"No! Refuse to acquiesce to mere statements, my dear friend. Attend closely, execute with precision, and assess with discernment! The Mind knows no equivocation. At present, behold the presence or absence of a thing! It is akin to a binary state in the rudimentary language of computers. In due course, you shall uncover the enigmatic quantum Supra-position of the Mind, wherein it can seemingly exist and not exist simultaneously in myriad 'places' or realities. All of this is made possible by its wondrous, illuminating power of undying Bodhi. The authentic Mind is Unborn, utterly pure, and exquisitely expressive in its creativity. Undoubtedly, it is through this Bodhipower that the enigma of the Tower at hand shall be resolved."

The Fourth Dhyana

Evan persisted in ruminating upon the irksome predicament before him, with a mind consumed by the weight of his thoughts.

"What is the underlying essence of this shrouded tower and what is the optimal approach to accessing its innermost sanctum?"

"Through careful observation while under the influence of the Fourth Dhyana", intoned his teacher.

"I have long been curious about the nature of the Fourth Dhyana or the fourth level of Dhyana. Please elaborate."

"The fourth level dhyana is the gateway to the illustrious Tathagata Ch'an, also known as the 'Black' Dragon Zen. Here, all phenomena are meticulously anteceded, and the Mind stands at the gateless gate of the dark principle of its true self. This level is aptly named, for it is here that one invites the supreme higher Bodhi of infinite Buddhas to awaken the sleeping Buddha from its great dream and unite with the great spiritual sangha of these Buddhas. In this state, one transcends the limitations of being a mere sattva or an inadequate idea seeking fulfillment in its own inadequate becoming. The sleeping 'Buddha' awakens to its true self, 'turning back' [paravritti] to itself through the discovery of this higher aspect of Bodhi, finding fulfillment [sukha] in itself AS SUCH [Tathata]. This mystical Union is a profound experience that can occur at any given moment. Therefore, one must train oneself to be prepared at all times, whether dreaming, walking, talking, or even in the great imagination of dying. When it arrives, it comes with great force, like a highly progressive and potent energy that seizes and paralyzes the body.

"Indeed, one cannot help but ponder the potential peril that may arise from such a circumstance. What if the occurrence transpires whilst an individual is navigating a motor vehicle? Such a scenario could prove to be quite precarious, would it not?"

"Do you truly believe that the enlightened Buddhas would deign to deprive this inadequate notion of its present fanciful existence, or the lives of other sentient beings? Such an act would be a gross interference in the dream of the slumbering, and would surely shatter the Buddhapath of proper awakening. The Buddhas are not mere Karma, my dear one. Nay, it is you who are Karma. Their boundless bodhipower never ceases to nourish this dream, yet the slumbering one remains blind and preoccupied with this illusory realm, filtered through the skandhas, unable to perceive the obscure light or power of Higher Bodhi. Instead of utilizing the lower aspect of Bodhi to focus the Mind into a state of prepared initiation, the slumbering one employs it to animate a false self - a self that is none other than YOU - replete with a host of false emotions, a lust for carnal pleasures, vain dreams of various sorts, self-induced problems, and so forth. How could even the mightiest of hammers shatter such vast foolishness of Bodhi? It takes great effort, right view, and a wise Teacher to dispel such an Illusion."

"I have gained a lucid comprehension of the approach required for this task. The knowledge I acquired from my initial attempt corroborates much of your teachings today. However, in a moment of vulnerability, my former tendencies ensnared me in the alluring melody of Mara's sirens. I humbly apologize."

"There is no need for apologies, my dear friend. Treat yourself with kindness in the present moment. Why subject yourself to torment? Instead, make a transformative shift in your mindset when it comes to detrimental habits. Convert these unwholesome practices into a source of wholesome and exultant determination and energy, propelling you towards a continuous and unwavering fourth level dhyana.

Come, let us venture forth into the resplendent realm of the Fourth Dhyana and finally unravel the enigma of this vexing tower."

With a gentle touch, the Ch'an Master graced Evan's head, igniting a familiar spark that liberated him from the oppressive burden of the skandhas...

The Twelve Holes of Karma

Suddenly, a realization of grandeur struck him with great force - he had been ensconced within the illustrious Tower all this time. Instead of the vast expanse of the sky, Evan was confronted with a radiant white ceiling. The sandy beach and far-off horizons were replaced by the curved white walls of the tower. His seating arrangement was no longer a weed-covered rock, but rather a sturdy stool crafted from pale steel. The circular area appeared to be vacant, with the exception of a central column that extended from the floor to the ceiling. However, the column's surface appeared to be unsteady, as if it were in a perpetual state of gradual motion, akin to smoke. The scene had been naught but a reverie, a mirage, a grandiose illusion foolishly perceived as veritable and perpetuated by the human psyche's yearning and lack of comprehension of the authentic essence of existence. Presently, there was now only an opulent emancipation from the constraints of time and space itself.

Evan's old teacher had vanished and emerging from the hazy mist, a gnome-like entity materialized. Its eyes lacked pupils, instead, they were hollowed out cavities that, if gazed upon for an extended duration, would consume the observer entirely, akin to the abyssal depths of a black hole.

"Please do not be alarmed by the absence of pupils in my eyes," stated the creature. "In fact, my visual acuity surpasses yours significantly. I possess the ability to perceive the vibrational essence of objects, which means that there is no distinction between myself and an object. I am able to sense its vibrational presence as if it were an extension of my own being. Furthermore, I possess the capability to perceive thought-forms that permeate the ether.

"Indeed, upon a closer inspection of the center of my ocular cavities, you will be able to discern the emergence of shapes that currently depict the narrative of humanity's sorrowful condition in the context of dependent origination.

"You shall gain insight into the creation and dissolution of worlds. Countless individuals in slumber shall be observed, envisioning themselves traversing, inhabiting, perishing, and undergoing rebirth in various forms within said worlds."

Evan was irresistibly drawn into the vast, swirling abyss of darkness nestled within the unfathomable depths of the creature's bottomless ocular cavities. Before him lay twelve individual karmic-holes, out of which emerged the eternal mass of ignorance that plagues the multitude of sentient beings, as the creature's mellifluous voice recounted the scene…

"As is evident, the karmic-holes depict images comprising twelve characters. One of these characters is a blind woman, symbolizing the feeling of ignorance. She navigates her surroundings with the aid of a stick, representing the spiritual blindness that often leads individuals to stumble through life. This stumbling creates a distorted perception of both oneself and the world, and directs one's will towards unreal pursuits. Consequently, one's character is shaped in accordance with this misguided direction of will, desire, and imagination.

"The next character is the potter, representing the creative force that shapes form. Just as a potter molds clay into a desired shape, we too mold our character and destiny, or karma, through our actions, words, and thoughts. These volitional acts become the cause of new activity and constitute the actively directing principle or character of a new consciousness. A character is merely a manifestation of our will, which is shaped by repeated actions. Each action leaves a trace, forming a path that we instinctively follow when faced with similar situations. This is known as the law of action and reaction, or karma, which dictates that we tend to move in the direction of least resistance - the path that has been frequently trodden and is therefore easier to follow. This is commonly referred to as the 'force of habit.'

"Just as a potter shapes vessels out of formless clay, we shape our future consciousness through our actions, words, and thoughts, using the still unformed material of our life and sense impressions. This consciousness gives form and direction to our future selves. When we depart from one life and enter into another, it is the consciousness that we have formed that serves as the nucleus or germ of our new embodiment.

"The third image depicts a monkey grasping a branch, symbolizing the restless nature of consciousness as it jumps from one object to another. It is important to note that consciousness cannot exist independently, as it continuously grasps sensory or imaginative objects and releases them for others. Additionally, consciousness has the ability to solidify and polarize into physical forms and mental functions. Ultimately, consciousness serves as the foundation for the combination of mind and body.

"The intimate correlation between bodily and mental functions is likened to two individuals in a boat, as illustrated in the fourth image featuring a ferryman propelling a vessel with two occupants. This psychophysical organism, comprising the mind and body, is further distinguished by the formation and operation of the six senses - sight, hearing, smell, taste, touch, and thought. These faculties are akin to the windows of a dwelling, through which we perceive the external world. They are depicted as a house with six windows. The sixth image symbolizes the interaction of the senses with their objects, akin to the initial encounter between lovers. The sensation arising from the contact of the senses with their objects is represented in the seventh image by a man whose eye has been pierced by an arrow.

"The eighth image depicts a patron being served a drink by a female attendant. This portrayal serves as a symbol of the yearning for life or desire instigated by pleasurable sensations. The arrow piercing the eye does not signify "pleasure," but rather the magnitude of the sensation and the potential for future painful consequences that may befall those who succumb to the allure of agreeable sensations.

"The desire for existence gives rise to the act of grasping and clinging onto desired objects. This phenomenon is represented in the ninth image, where a man is depicted plucking fruit from a tree and collecting it in a basket. The act of clinging reinforces the limitations of life and initiates a new cycle of transformation, as symbolized by the sexual union of a man and woman in the tenth image.

"The eleventh image depicts a woman in the process of delivering a child. The act of becoming ultimately results in a rebirth into a new existence. The twelfth image depicts a man carrying a corpse, which is wrapped in cloth according to Tibetan tradition, on his back to the cremation ground or the place where deceased bodies are disposed of. This image serves to illustrate the final link in the formula of dependent origination, which states that all that is born leads to old age and death.

"The Buddha began his inquiry with a simple question: 'What is it that makes old age and death possible?' The answer was that, due to being born, we experience old age and death. If there had not been a will to live and a clinging to the corresponding forms of life, this process of becoming would not have been initiated."

Evan confidently stated, "Although I am aware of the veracity of this information, it appears to be excessively harsh, do you not agree?"

"Indeed, as they explicate, the attachment that we experience is a result of craving, an insatiable "thirst" for the objects of sensory pleasure. This craving, in turn, is conditioned by feeling, which discerns agreeable and disagreeable sensations. It is important to note that feeling can only arise through the contact of the senses with their corresponding objects. The senses are based on a psychophysical organism, and this organism can only arise if there is consciousness. However, consciousness, in our individually limited form, is conditioned by individual, egocentric activity that has occurred during countless previous forms of existence. Such activity is only possible as long as we are ensnared in the illusion of our separate ego-hood."

Evan emphatically stated that it is all a vicious cycle.

"The twelve-fold formula of dependent origination is represented as a circle because it has no beginning or end. Each link represents the sum total of all other links and is both the precondition and outcome of all other links. All phases of this dependent origination are phenomena of the same illusion - the illusion of egohood.

"Such is the reality of these twelve apertures, and henceforth, I shall proceed to seal them."

With a mischievous glint in his eye, the impish creature sprang to his feet and, with the grace of a master artisan, expertly sealed every last hole into oblivion, leaving no trace of their existence.

The Ubiquitous Edifice

The remarkable accomplishment of sealing the karmic voids left Evan in a state of astonishment.

"Indeed, you possess the extraordinary ability to dissolve and absolve the relentless cycle of the karmadhatu. Pray tell, how might such a feat be accomplished?"

The mischievous being responded with a sly grin, "Kindly lend me your ear, and I shall narrate a story that is truly remarkable to contemplate. "Long ago, I was trapped in a defensive state of mind that kept me isolated from the cosmos. My thoughts were filled with outdated words, and my emotions were stifled by hardened feelings that overshadowed my every heartbeat, preventing any light from shining through. My desire for life had turned into a prison, consuming me and leaving me feeling lost without purpose. In despising myself and cutting myself off from others, I found myself in this dark tower, questioning who I truly was. I was nothing more than a lonely figure, lost in my own ego. But then, without warning, a powerful force emerged both within and around me - the omnipotent power that unites all entities in perfect harmony. It was as if a floodgate had opened, allowing the energy of both Heaven and the physical world to flow through me like a storm. I experienced the intensity of the Earth's core and the brilliance of the universe's center. I became a conduit, no longer merely an inhabitant of the tower. And then, the joy of unity burst forth. The high became low, and the low became high. I understood that everything trapped in the physical world flowed through me. I, the epitome of grandeur, stood as the central pillar of a celestial dance. I was nothing short of the human form, basking in the radiance of its primordial energy.

"The enigma of the tower, struck by a thunderbolt from the heavens, compels me to declare its significance and import with utmost clarity, in order to leave an indelible impression on all those who seek profound truths.

"As this truth takes hold, flashes of insight beckon one to embrace change. Having achieved great feats and attained a profound understanding, one is now summoned to a higher calling. This calling demands that one break free from the confines of old structures and experience life anew. It is the very essence of Satori: the ultimate expression of unbridled freedom, where the mind is liberated and the true essence of the Self is unveiled and comprehended. This profound realization awakens the very nature of existence itself. A crucial element in attaining satori is the art of acceptance."

Evan inquired, "And so you ventured forth to bask in the glory of your True and Undivided Self amidst this unfettered ocean of vice?"

"Verily so," replied the impish creature. "The Tower itself remains the perpetual source of my strength and ability to shape phenomena to my will."

Evan responded with awe, stating, "It appears to possess qualities akin to those of a living organism."

"Indeed, it is accurate to state that it appears as though the voice of the Tower itself once communicated with me.

"I possess the spiritual energy that liberates the imprisoned inner-self, enabling it to ascend to greater fulfillment. The sudden immersion into an alternate state of awareness can be a liberating experience, even if its significance is not immediately apparent. At times my apparent upheaval can also dismantle spiritual arrogance, breaking down the barriers of outdated creeds and dogmas, and propelling you towards new, intuitive, and vibrant spiritual pursuits."
"It is intriguing to contemplate the most effective means of harnessing the spiritual energy within oneself," responded Evan."

"Quite right. Meditation itself is the noble and valiant endeavor of the "lower self" to harmonize with the "higher Self" in the divine radiance. As concentration is a prerequisite to meditation, so does the latter inevitably lead to contemplation, a transition from reflection and dialogue to the stillness and utter silence of a supernatural communion in the Unborn. In this state, one no longer merely ponders from afar, but rather, the very essence of the matter is present and reveals itself. Contemplation is the fusion of the thinker with reality, where one does not arrive at a 'conclusion,' but rather, one receives - or rather, experiences - the imprint of Reality itself.

"Finally, the Tower experience strikes with the ferocity of a lightning bolt, shattering the outdated hierarchies of the past. It is said that the Tower embodies the opulent interpretation of the cosmos, while the lightning symbolizes the destruction that befalls a life built solely on materialistic principles. The mystics proclaim that revelation reveals itself in a sudden and potent lightning bolt that eradicates the illusions of the physical realm in a single, awe-inspiring moment. This phenomenon is akin to the transformative experiences of Paul on his journey to Damascus or the one that struck Buddha while meditating under the Bodhi tree."

Evan found himself standing in solitary silence amidst a revelation that filled him with a sense of reverence and wonder.

Starship Unbound

Disembarking from the enigmatic tower, a peculiar sensation overcame Evan as a fiery tremble coursed through his entire body. His heart accelerated its rhythm, and the mind was consumed by tumultuous thoughts. He became acutely aware of the presence of portentous mysteries that surrounded him. Soon after, beams of light penetrated his very being, illuminating many things that had previously been shrouded in darkness, of whose existence Evan had been unaware. Veils were lifted, and whispers of wisdom echoed in his ears, causing all previous knowledge to take on a new and different meaning. He discovered a symphony of connections between disparate elements, previously thought to be unrelated. Objects that were once distant and dissimilar now appeared close and similar. In the sky, a colossal star appeared, surrounded by seven smaller stars whose rays intermingled, filling space with immeasurable radiance and splendor.

Upon realization, Evan was enraptured by the celestial realm of which the great Plotinus spoke: A place where all is diaphanous, where darkness and resistance are but a distant memory, and where clarity reigns supreme. Every facet of this ethereal plane is laid bare, visible to all who seek it, both within and without. Light begets light, as all things contain within themselves the essence of all else, and in turn, perceive all things in one another. Thus, all is everywhere, and all is one. Each entity, no matter how small, is imbued with the grandeur of infinity. The splendor of this realm is boundless, for even the most minuscule of elements is endowed with greatness beyond measure. Yea, starship unbound.

In a hushed tone, a melodious voice gently caressed his ear.

"Your authentic journey is now commencing once again. By engaging in introspection, you are now able to perceive veracity. You can comprehend your inherent disposition and your place in the cosmos. This awareness empowers you to alter your manner of self-articulation. By comprehending your True Nature, you are capable of having faith in yourself, and thus adjust and regulate your conduct in accordance with your own intuition. At present, there is no longer a necessity to justify yourself or to behave defensively as you have done previously. You may withdraw serenely. You may rest in quietude. All of your progress has been achieved through introspection. You have engaged in reflection during moments of tranquility and contemplation in periods of silence. You have successfully subdued the disruptive impact of external noise and eliminated distractions.

"One has acquired this knowledge through the trials and tribulations of both their current and past lives. The journey has been arduous, marked by repeated encounters with the destruction of what was once believed to be the ultimate truth, as well as the wreckage of one's own life. The very foundations of one's existence have been repeatedly shattered. However, throughout these experiences, nothing essential has been forfeited or abandoned. Each experience has contributed to one's growth and transformation, ultimately leading to a sense of wholeness. At times, setbacks may have been perceived as regression, but in reality, they were merely a transition to a more demanding level of Self-realization.

"Your Unborn Mind is ascending. You have discovered the commencement of the veracious path. You are traversing the route towards eternal Bodhi-delight. You have reconciled with your inner being and comprehended that all corporeal entities are ephemeral. Every form must be surpassed and relinquished. The everlasting existence and illumination are situated within the inner realm. You have acquired this gnosis by shifting the focus of your mind's gaze from the observation of superficiality to the supraperception of Actuality. You have realized that it is imperative to pursue your own destiny in Light of the Unborn.

"If the tower was the disruptive force that shattered the illusion of security, then the star serves as a source of inspiration and guidance to rebuild with a heightened perspective. It represents the stabilization and tranquility that follows the revelations brought about by the tower. Metaphorically, the Star embodies the ethereal mentor that we bear within, who is inextricably linked to the most profound energies of the cosmos and to the divine. It represents the enigmatic facet of our being, in which we can place our trust: our "fortunate star." Seek sanctuary within its embrace. Its luminosity shall guide you towards further uncharted realms of the Unborn."

A Most Luminous Light

As Evan's arduous journey pressed on, he found himself confronted with a desolate plain that stretched out before him, a barren and bleak expanse that seemed to have been forsaken by the very gods themselves. The full moon, radiant and resplendent in all her glory, cast a contemplative gaze upon the land, as if hesitant to unveil the secrets that lay hidden within. Under the moon's wavering light, the shadows seemed to come alive, dancing and swaying in their own peculiar rhythm, as if they possessed a life of their own.

In the distance, Evan's eyes were drawn to the majestic blue hills that stood proudly, their peaks reaching towards the heavens. Between these towering grey structures, a winding path stretched out, seemingly leading to a destination far beyond the reaches of his sight. It was a path that beckoned him forward, promising adventure and mystery.

Yet, as Evan approached the path, he noticed two figures that sat on either side, their presence adding an eerie aura to the already haunting scene. A wolf and a dog, their silhouettes illuminated by the moon's ethereal glow, sat and howled at the night sky. Their mournful cries echoed through the stillness, sending a chill down Evan's spine. He recalled the ancient belief that dogs possess an uncanny ability to sense the presence of thieves and ghosts, and a shiver ran down his spine, causing his heart to quicken its pace.

Just as Evan's unease began to settle in, a sudden movement caught his attention. From a nearby rivulet, a large black crab emerged, its claws clicking against the sand as it made its way towards him. The sight of this unexpected visitor only added to the eerie atmosphere that surrounded him. A heavy, cold dew began to fall, dampening the ground beneath his feet and further intensifying the sense of foreboding that hung in the air.

With each passing moment, Evan felt himself being drawn deeper into this enigmatic landscape, his curiosity and trepidation intertwining like the shadows that danced before him. Little did he know that this desolate plain held secrets that would challenge his very perception of reality, and that his journey was far from finished.

Dread consumed Evan, his heart pounding in his chest, as he became acutely aware of the existence of a mysterious realm. It was a world teeming with malevolent spirits, where corpses clawed their way out of their graves and wailing ghosts roamed freely. The pale moonlight cast an eerie glow upon the scene, intensifying the feeling of being watched by unseen eyes lurking behind the towering structures.

Evan's instincts screamed at him to keep moving forward, to resist the temptation of looking back into the shadows. He knew all too well the dangers that awaited him there. Yet, as if in defiance of his fear, the radiant luminosity of the full moon managed to penetrate his apprehensions. Its ethereal glow seemed to cast a protective shield around him, causing a faint smile to grace the moon's silvery countenance.

In that fleeting moment, Evan's attention was abruptly diverted by a sound that seemed to emanate from the very fabric of the night. It was a voice, so enchanting and melodious, that it sent shivers down his spine. The dulcet tones gently caressed his ears, whispering words that seemed to carry a hidden message. It was the most captivating voice he had ever encountered, and it held him spellbound.

As the whispered words reached his ears, Evan felt a strange mixture of fear and fascination. The voice seemed to possess an otherworldly quality, as if it belonged to a being from a realm beyond human comprehension. Its words were laden with a mysterious power, drawing him closer to the edge of his own reality.

Unable to resist the allure any longer, Evan turned his gaze towards the source of the voice. What he saw defied all logic and reason. Standing before him was a figure cloaked in darkness, yet emanating a faint glow that seemed to dance in harmony with the moonlight. It was a being of ethereal beauty, with eyes that held the secrets of a thousand lifetimes.

In that moment, Evan's fear was momentarily forgotten, replaced by an overwhelming curiosity. He felt an inexplicable connection to this enigmatic being, as if they were bound by a thread that transcended time and space. The voice continued to weave its enchanting spell, drawing him further into its web of mystery.

"Our initial encounter took place within the realm of my enigmatic relative, the Primordial. At that time, you were still in pursuit of external sources of wisdom. Nevertheless, due to the subsequent experiences you have undergone, it is evident that you now comprehend that the very essence of what you seek resides within you, and has always been an inseparable component of your being. One's vision of the future may be obscured, yet it is imperative to remain steadfast on the chosen path. Place your trust in intuition, for in the depths of despair, you shall discover the radiance of your own inner light. Allow this light to illuminate the shadows of fear, and in doing so, you shall be propelled towards a greater understanding of self, imbued with strength and self-assurance.

"Amidst the trials and tribulations that beset you, you found yourself questioning, 'Why must I endure such hardships?' Yet, in the depths of your despair, profound revelations emerged. Ideas, like ethereal specters, ascended from the depths of your consciousness. Just when you believed you could bear no more, another ordeal presented itself, and yet you persisted. You pressed on, unwavering in your determination, and in doing so, new thoughts blossomed forth. New pathways, previously unseen, materialized before your very eyes. Time has been spent in deep contemplation and envisioning, resulting in profound spiritual awakening.

"Under the solemn radiance of my luminosity, your intuition now reigns supreme. You have kept the mystical aspects of your being confined, but as the Moon ascends, these facets are set free. At a certain juncture, when guided by the Unborn's influence, we begin to reflect on our past and realize that our journey thus far has been right and just. We come to comprehend that there is nothing truly novel under the Sun, and that everything is unfolding as it should. We perceive that while the river of life may appear to be in constant motion, forever changing and presenting new experiences, it remains unchanged at its core. It seems to flow aimlessly, yet possesses a certain consistency, a certain endurance. It remains the same in both triumph and defeat. This river, in all its sameness, holds a profound significance. To those with the ability to perceive, every step taken within this river of life becomes sacred ground.

"Certainly, akin to the celestial presence of the moon positioned overhead, the Buddha Mind or one's authentic essence embodies a parallel significance. How do we attain this Self-realization? We reach this juncture by consciously undergoing and forming a connection with the formidable challenges we face. Each trial then becomes a rite of passage, enabling us to progress to the subsequent stage. La Luna represents the ultimate initiation into divine darkness. It signifies the final symbolic demise, succeeded by a divine rebirth in the Unborn. You are currently in the concluding phase of a sequence of trials.

"What sets apart the commencement of this opulent day from its predecessors? It is the recognition of your mind's independent odyssey. It is the cognizance that every formidable impediment encountered on your journey served as a test of your fortitude and tenacity. It constituted an appraisal of your spiritual prowess, determination, and proficiency. In the opulent rite of your divine initiation, your corporeal form transcends into a luminous entity. In this sacred ceremony, you relinquish the weight of your past and embrace the celestial effulgence bestowed upon you by a superior evolutionary manifestation. The everlasting radiance permeates your divine essence, as if you are reaching towards the heavens, accepting and comprehending. The hands of divinity envelop you in their embrace, imbuing you with the enchanting seeds of sagacity. You can never revert to your former self, for the rite of passage is consummated. You have metamorphosed into the very fount of Unborn Light. Svaha."

An Arcanum of Intuition

As I continued my journey along the winding road, a breathtaking scene unfolded before my eyes. The once gloomy sky had transformed into a canvas of vibrant colors, as the heavy clouds gracefully dispersed, allowing the radiant sun to cast its golden rays upon the horizon. The road ahead seemed to glow with an ethereal luminosity, beckoning me to venture further.

As I approached a clearing in the distance, my heart quickened with anticipation. At the center of this enchanting space stood a magnificent podium, seemingly carved out of the very essence of beauty itself. Its grandeur was unparalleled, commanding attention and admiration from all who laid eyes upon it.

But it was not the podium alone that captivated my senses; it was what adorned it that truly took my breath away. A resplendent tablet, gleaming with an otherworldly brilliance, was perched atop the podium as if it were a sacred relic. Its surface seemed to radiate a celestial energy, as if it held within it the secrets of the universe.

The tablet, a masterpiece of craftsmanship, was a sight to behold. Its elegant design and intricate etchings spoke of a profound wisdom and ancient knowledge. It was as if the tablet itself was a living entity, pulsating with a divine power that resonated with the very core of my being.

As I drew closer, the inscription on the tablet came into focus. The words, delicately etched into the surface, seemed to dance before my eyes, inviting me to decipher their hidden meaning. With bated breath, I began to read the elegantly unfolded message.

The enigmatic essence of intuition lies within the realm of illuminating innocence, unveiling profound wisdom. It bestows upon the soul an unwavering gaze, untroubled by the shadows of uncertainty and the hesitations born from it. It is the divine vision that perceives reality in its unadulterated form, basking under the eternal radiance of a new dawn. This sacred knowledge imparts the art of surrendering to the pure and unadorned impressions that effortlessly unveil the essence of existence. It transcends the realm of intellectual conjectures and elaborate constructs, allowing the truth of things to manifest in their unfiltered splendor. To elevate impressions to a realm beyond the mundane, this is the essence of the Arcanum "The Sun," the embodiment of intuitive revelation.

The exquisite Arcanum of intuition lies in the art of elevating the reflective intelligence to the realm of creative brilliance. It is the harmonious fusion of this enlightened intelligence with profound wisdom, a magnificent endeavor that entails the restoration of the celestial bond between the diminished light of earthly intellect and the resplendent radiance of celestial knowledge. Once this celestial union is achieved, the reawakened intelligence shall be united with the divine wisdom, transcending mortal limitations and embracing the Unborn essence.

Evan's internal mentor subsequently addressed him in the following manner:

"Behold, a revelation dawns upon you! The brilliance of enlightenment illuminates your path, as you emerge into a realm of resplendence. It becomes clear to you that you have traversed a celestial conduit, guided by divine agencies towards profound realization. Now, you bask in the radiance of beauty, for in this realization, you are reborn amidst a luminous aura. Every facet of your being, both the luminous and the obscure, harmoniously intertwine. Your fears, once overwhelming, now find their rightful place in the grand tapestry of existence. Every aspect of your being merges seamlessly with the celestial light that permeates the cosmos.

"The eternal radiance of the divine cosmos becomes an integral part of your essence, forever intertwined. The divine light, everlasting and unyielding, transcends the ephemeral darkness that may momentarily shroud your path. The transient movements of the mortal vessel pale in comparison to the profound gnosis you have attained. Through this awakening, you experience a spiritual rebirth, a metamorphosis of the soul.

"One is reborn by achieving a state of singularity in both mind and spirit. This state of singularity allows one to perceive the imageless countenance of the Unborn, thereby transcending all limitations. As stated by Jesus in Matthew 6:22, 'The light of the body is the eye: if therefore thine eye be single, thy whole body shall be full of light.' You have truly embarked on a remarkable journey of self-transformation. Your unwavering dedication to following the Lankavatarian ten-fold path to Noble Self-realization is truly commendable. You have shown great perseverance in cultivating:

Right Understanding: In recognizing the inherent truth that all that is brought into existence, conceived, and undergoes transformation is ultimately destined to deteriorate and cease to exist, it can be concluded that the process of birth, conception, and becoming of any phenomenon is inherently characterized by suffering for a Mind that clings to these phenomena. The underlying principle here lies in the fact that the Mind becomes subservient to that which it pursues.

Right Mindfulness: The emergence of this concept stems from a profound comprehension within a particular state of consciousness, wherein a commitment is made to refrain from blindly adhering to external phenomena. Instead, the focus is on cultivating the ability to transcend the ingrained patterns of dependence that arise in relation to these phenomena. Consequently, it is imperative for the mind to take precedence over all external occurrences, so as to liberate itself from servitude and attain the rightful status of self-awakened mastery.

Right Speech: A discerning intellect, one that comprehends the potency of causality and the unceasing origin that sustains this principle, is cognizant of the perilous consequences that may arise if it fails to exercise prudence in its expressions. Essentially, it enlightens the intellect that hitherto it has been "reactive" to what it has deemed as tangible and vastly disparate from its ephemeral being.

Right Action: The correct perspective is held by a mind that has realized that the root cause of its previous reactions and consequent suffering is essentially the same essence that acted upon its desires and delusions. This mind has discovered that the true actor is inherently deathless, radiant, profoundly comprehensible, self-evident, effortlessly perfect, and entirely free from the taint of fear, arrogance, desire, avarice, and ignorance.

Right Living: The thought that now enters this Mind is one of awakening. Until now, it has nurtured various desires to find a temporary dwelling. It has sought convenient justifications to live a comfortable life in a mortal body, and for this body, it has sought a suitable refuge to find peace and fulfill its desires. However, with a correct understanding of the Unborn Mind, which requires no dwelling and has no need for a physical abode, this Mind has now embraced the obscure principle of existing in that which precedes all dwellings. This Mind has entered the initial stage of equilibrium and serenity, even in the midst of chaos.

Right Effort: The current state of affairs for such a Mind entails a profound understanding of the realities within the realms of internal and external phenomena. It possesses a limited number of illusions regarding the world and recognizes the detrimental consequences that have arisen from the previous veneration of deceptive deities such as fear, pride, desire, greed, and ignorance. These misguided practices have inflicted considerable suffering upon it and fostered the development of numerous unfavorable habits. Consequently, this Mind directs its attention towards that which is genuine, while consciously evading the allure of falsehoods. It diligently avoids engaging in habitual patterns that lead to suffering and instead strives for transformation into a more wholesome existence.

Right Faith: Through diligent study, examination, and assessment of what has been discovered as truth, the notion of gotra (Bodhi-seed) is comprehended and embraced, leading to a state of enduring bliss. This acquisition of faith subsequently prompts a deeper exploration and contemplation of this enigmatic principle, which had previously eluded understanding due to the captivating influence of external or internal phenomena.

Right Concentration: (Dhyana) Now, the Mind has transformed into a vibrant and joyful actuality. It comprehends the age-old adage that states, "the reality of the Mind is shaped by its focal point." Consequently, it directs its attention towards that which remains impervious to deterioration, corruption, or any form of distortion, namely the gotra.

Through proper concentration on this eternal source of wisdom, one attains the fourth level of dhyana and progresses further until reaching the level of Tathagata dhyana. At this stage, one becomes aware of the illuminating light of the Unborn Mind, which precedes and animates the false reality perceived by countless sentient beings who are influenced by the five great thieves (skhandas). One also discovers the highest manifestation of bodhipower in the Unborn Mind, which is inherently empty yet capable of instantaneously animating any form or formless state. Furthermore, one realizes the interconnectedness between this illusory dual state and all minds that are captivated by its ever-changing reflections. With this profound insight, one uncovers...

Right Gnosis: Having acquired the appropriate knowledge, it has reached an irreversible stage. At present, it is liberated from the afflictions and perpetual cycle of transformation caused by ignorance and the belief in a mortal existence, namely the physical body. It takes delight in the euphoric liberation bestowed by the boundless creative potential of the Unborn Mind, and consequently, it unearths its authentic essence as nothing but its inherent nature, known as Tathata. Henceforth, it can genuinely proclaim itself as truly awakened and eternally emancipated from the constraints of ignorance and suffering. It patiently awaits the opportune moment of:

Right Release: After having regained the correct understanding of its true nature, which the Lankavatarians often refer to as Noble Wisdom, the entity has come to realize what was always present but previously obscured by defilements - Buddhahood. It now comprehends that a Buddha can never be born and therefore can never die. The Mind that truly embodies a Buddha is thus perfectly Unborn. It recognizes that the true nature of a Buddha Mind is a supra-consciousness of sheer productivity, or creative light, which illuminates all ten directions and is therefore the creator of all countless Minds that desire to remain as sentient beings due to ignorance and inadequate ideas. It understands that it can manifest before any such Mind through infinite Bodhisattvic aspects, or awakened ideas. To such a Mind, the body is now perceived as a mere illusion, a bubble in the water of infinite creative light. This Mind can now free itself from this bubble at any given moment and "join" the most radiant and compassionate truth that encompasses all suffering minds that still cling to the idea of becoming and conditioning and are blind to the unbecoming and unconditioned nirvana element known as Noble Wisdom…

"You have now verified the ultimate reality or the Unborn Mind.

"Hence, the exquisite Arcanum of intuition is that of revelatory naivety in the act of Self-gnosis, which endows the spirit with an intensity of gaze untroubled by doubt and the scruples that doubt engenders. It is the vision of things as they truly are, basking in the eternal radiance of the sun's new day. This Arcanum teaches the art of surrendering oneself to the pure and simple impressions that reveal the essence of things, unencumbered by intellectual hypotheses and superstructures. To imbue these impressions with a numinous quality is the very essence of the Arcanum 'The Sun', the Arcanum of intuition."

Part Two

Dark Sessions

In the early evening mist, Pamela, a young woman in her early twenties, stood at the foot of a hill, her heart pounding with a mix of excitement and trepidation. She had recently embarked on a career as a paranormal investigator, and the assignment that lay before her was unlike anything she had encountered before. It was the peculiar mansion, perched atop the hill that beckoned her with its enigmatic presence.

As she gazed up at the aged dwelling, Pamela couldn't help but feel a shiver run down her spine. The legend surrounding the mansion was one of the most haunting she had ever heard. It was said that within those decaying walls, a sickly child with an abnormally enlarged and eerie head had once resided. The mere thought of it chilled her to the bone.

The child, according to the tales passed down through generations, was said to have spent its days in the Tower Room, perpetually peering through the misty windowpane. The image of its chilling silhouette, cast against the foggy glass, had become a symbol of both fear and fascination for those who dared to venture near the mansion.

Pamela's knowledge of the legend was rudimentary at best, but it only fueled her curiosity further. She yearned to uncover the truth behind the stories that had haunted the mansion for so long. With her trusty equipment in hand, she took a deep breath and began her ascent up the hill, determined to face whatever awaited her within those mysterious walls.

As she climbed higher, the wind whispered through the trees, adding an eerie soundtrack to her journey. The mansion loomed larger with each step, its presence becoming more palpable. Pamela's heart raced, her mind filled with a mix of anticipation and fear. What secrets lay hidden within those walls? What had become of the child with the abnormally enlarged head?

Pamela stood at the threshold of the old, creaky door, her heart pounding with anticipation. She had been waiting for this moment for what felt like an eternity. She had heard so much about Agnes, her esteemed compatriot in the realm of the supernatural, and she couldn't wait to finally meet her.

As she pushed the door open, she was greeted by a dimly lit room, filled with the scent of incense and the sound of soft chanting. And there, standing before her, was Agnes herself. Pamela couldn't believe her eyes. She had heard so much about Agnes, but seeing her in person was something else entirely.

A brief introduction to Agnes is warranted. At approximately sixty years of age, she possessed a moderate stature accompanied by a robust physique, complemented by her silvery-white hair. Wire-rimmed glasses were securely perched on her nose, and her keen, eagle-like eyes possessed an uncanny ability to penetrate through one's very being. Agnes, a woman of German ancestry, exhibited a gentle demeanor, unless provoked. However, she was far from being an ordinary investigator. Having dedicated years to the pursuit of truth, she ascended to the esteemed rank of "Master" in the spiritual discipline of "Unknowing." To comprehend the path that leads to the ultimate inquiries and resolutions of all matters, one must first relinquish all preconceived knowledge, for the source that underlies everything remains beyond the realm of comprehension. Adorning her neck was a silver medallion, bearing the depiction of a tree, its intricate roots delving deep into the earth, while its branches extended outward from its core. Rumor has it, within exclusive circles, that a "new branch" materializes each time Agnes guides an individual, who seeks her aid, safely through their personal journey of darkness and uncertainty.

Agnes, her noble superior in the realm of the occult and supernatural, had welcomed her with open arms earlier that evening. The esteemed woman's presence exuded an air of authority and wisdom, leaving Pamela in awe of her vast knowledge. Their customary exchanges had been filled with intrigue and mystique, as they delved into the secrets of the unknown.

But now, as the night wore on, Pamela found herself plagued by restlessness. Time seemed to stretch on endlessly, each minute feeling like an eternity. The silence of the room was broken only by the soft rustling of the curtains, as if the very fabric of the night whispered secrets to her.

Thoughts and questions swirled in Pamela's mind, like a tempestuous storm threatening to consume her. The mysteries of the occult, the supernatural forces that Agnes had dedicated her life to understanding, danced before her eyes. She yearned to unravel their enigmatic nature, to grasp the elusive truths that lay hidden in the shadows.

Pamela was gracefully escorted up a grandiose staircase that exuded opulence, leading her to a lavishly adorned bedroom that eagerly awaited her presence on the second floor. After bidding Agnes a goodnight, Pamela retired for the evening.

As the hours ticked by, Pamela's restlessness grew more pronounced. The weight of the unknown pressed upon her, suffocating her in its grip. She longed for the solace of sleep, for respite from the ceaseless thoughts that tormented her. But sleep eluded her, slipping through her fingers like sand in an hourglass.

Pamela lay in her bed, tossing and turning, unable to find any respite from her restlessness. The minutes stretched into hours, and it felt as though time itself had become interminable. Frustration gnawed at her, urging her to abandon the futile pursuit of sleep and rise from her bed.

Just as she was contemplating giving in to her restlessness and turning on the light, a faint, muffled sound reached her ears. It seemed to be coming from above, from the ceiling. Curiosity piqued, Pamela strained her ears, trying to make out the source of the sound. Gradually, it grew louder, and then, to her surprise, she heard three distinct knocks at the headrest of her bed.

Startled, Pamela jolted upright, her heart pounding in her chest. What could possibly be causing these strange sounds? As she pondered this question, her eyes were drawn to the adjacent wall. To her astonishment, it began to shift, ever so slowly, revealing a hidden staircase leading up to the Tower Room of the mansion.

A gentle, blue-green light emanated from the staircase, casting an ethereal glow on the surroundings. Pamela's mind raced with questions. Who could be summoning her to ascend this mysterious staircase? What secrets awaited her in the Tower Room?

With cautious steps, she approached the base of the staircase, her eyes fixed on the darkness above. As she peered upwards, straining to see through the deepening shadows, she thought she could make out two eyes gazing down at her. They seemed to burn into her very soul, drawing nearer and nearer with each passing moment.

A sense of paralysis began to creep over Pamela, threatening to immobilize her completely. But with a surge of remaining strength, she fought against the encroaching fear and swiftly moved to the corner of the room. In one swift motion, she switched on the light, flooding the space with brightness.

And there, before her, stood a sight that chilled her. It was a deformed child, its head bulbous and misshapen. It attempted to shield its eyes from the light with what appeared to be hands, its movements restricted and contorted. It resembled a twisted mass of tissue, an inverted human body. It endeavored to open what must have been a mouth, but before it could succeed, Pamela succumbed to unconsciousness.

Gradually awakening from her harrowing encounter, Pamela sensed a resurgence of her bravery and resilience the moment Agnes entered the room and approached her bedside.

As Pamela began to recount her harrowing encounter, her voice trembled slightly, betraying the residual fear that still lingered within her. Agnes listened intently, her eyes filled with a mixture of compassion and curiosity. The room seemed to hold its breath as Pamela described the nameless horror that had invaded her sanctuary, its grotesque appearance etched vividly in her memory.

As she spoke, Pamela's words painted a vivid picture of the terror she had experienced. The creature's presence had been suffocating, its malevolence palpable in the air. It had approached her with an eerie determination, its twisted form contorting in unnatural ways. Pamela's heart had raced, her body frozen with fear as the creature attempted to communicate in a language she couldn't comprehend.

Agnes listened, her grip on Pamela's hand tightening, offering a silent reassurance. She could feel the weight of Pamela's fear, the residual trauma that clung to her like a shadow. But Agnes also sensed something else within Pamela's words - a resilience, a strength that had been awakened by the encounter. It was as if the darkness had inadvertently ignited a flame within Pamela, reminding her of her own bravery.

As Pamela finished recounting her ordeal, there was a moment of silence that hung in the air. Agnes looked into Pamela's eyes, seeing the flicker of fear that had briefly resurfaced. Without hesitation, she clasped Pamela's hand firmly, offering her unwavering support. In that simple gesture, Agnes conveyed her belief in Pamela's strength, her unwavering trust.

The room seemed to brighten as Pamela's face transformed, a wide smile spreading across her features. It was a smile that radiated joy and gratitude, a testament to the profound impact Agnes had on her. In that moment, Pamela realized that she was not alone in her journey. Agnes, with her enigmatic presence and the ancient Tree medallion adorning her neck, had become a beacon of hope, a guiding light in the darkness.

Their conversation continued, the sacred bond of trust between them growing stronger with each passing word. Agnes shared her own experiences, her own battles with fear and adversity. And as they spoke, they discovered a shared spiritual depth, a connection that transcended the limitations of their current circumstances.

There was an enigmatic quality about this woman, adorned with the ancient Tree medallion that allowed Pamela to transcend the limitations imposed by her current circumstances.

Pamela's face briefly displayed a flicker of fear, which swiftly dissipated when Agnes clasped her hand. Subsequently, Pamela recounted the nameless horror that had invaded her room earlier that evening, along with her profound trepidation when the grotesque creature attempted to communicate.

"It is currently positioned above us, Agnes, attentively listening to our every word. The question arises: why is it in that location? However, more importantly, what is its purpose in relation to me?"

Agnes contorted her face into a deep frown, then directed her gaze towards Pamela. "To comprehend its intentions, you must first UNKNOW your fear of its existence, my dear."

"What do you mean, Agnes?"

"Do you have faith in me, Pamela?" inquired Agnes, gently adjusting her glasses to establish direct eye contact.

"Yes, Agnes, I cannot explain why, but I do."

"In that case, let go and trust as I guide you through a Dark Session."

Pamela closed her eyes and relied on the soothing sound of Agnes' voice. "Agnes, may I inquire about the meaning of a 'Dark Session'?"

"Simply put, it is a time to cast aside all fears and uncertainties, allowing them to be dissipated through a Cloud of Forgetfulness. Do not let anything disturb you; do not let anything frighten you. Everything is transient, but the great good remains constant, always present and comforting you. The good is akin to darkness to our senses, as we cannot fully comprehend its essence. All that we experience is merely a shadow of it, and when you find yourself enveloped by that shadow, it signifies that the presence of the good is nearby, safeguarding and favoring you."

"I am not entirely following, Agnes...you are starting to lose me..."

"Do not fret. Simply remember the aspect of letting go and trusting in a manner that is beyond your understanding. Learn to UNKNOW everything. Here is something that may assist you, listen:

Go, without knowledge of the destination;
Bring, without knowledge of what to bring;
The path is lengthy, the route unfamiliar;
One will discover how to arrive
There on their own;
One possesses the guidance and assistance
Of higher forces of goodness...

"Can you remember that?"

"I believe so. Would you be willing to assist me once more?"

"Certainly. However, when I do, I request that you 'rise' and follow me without opening your eyes, regardless of where the unknown path may lead. Do you comprehend?"

"Yes, I am willing."

In what felt like a mere blink of an eye, Pamela's eyes fluttered open, and she found herself standing in the Tower Room. The room was dimly lit, with a haunting atmosphere that sent shivers down her spine. But this time, there was something different. In one of the corners, the nameless entity that had caused her such terror before was crouched, its presence undeniable.

However, to Pamela's surprise, fear was not the emotion that coursed through her veins. Instead, she felt an overwhelming desire to reach out and provide comfort to the entity. It was as if a newfound understanding had washed over her, erasing any remnants of fear that had once consumed her.

"Are you present with me, Agnes?" Pamela whispered, her voice barely audible in the eerie silence of the room.

"Yes, Pamela," Agnes replied, her voice filled with a sense of calm assurance. "I am in close proximity. I also see the entity. She is responding to you and wishes to accept your touch."

Pamela's brows furrowed in confusion. "She? How can that be? It is not human."

Agnes paused for a moment, as if contemplating how to explain the inexplicable. "She is partially human and partially something else," she finally responded. "She's also an empath, capable of feeling and understanding emotions on a profound level. Allow her to reveal the other part to you. It is acceptable to do so. You may approach and touch her."

With newfound courage, Pamela took a deep breath and calmly approached the entity. As she extended her arms, a surge of anticipation coursed through her. The entity, sensing her intentions, immediately embraced her, its touch radiating a warmth that only a mother could provide. It was a warmth that had been lacking in both their lives for far too long.

In that moment, something extraordinary happened. Their consciousnesses merged, intertwining their thoughts and emotions into a unified whole. All cognitive faculties ceased to exist, leaving only an overwhelming exchange of profound empathy between them. It was as if they were two souls, finally finding solace and understanding in each other's presence.

Time seemed to stand still as they remained locked in their embrace, their connection growing stronger with each passing moment. The Tower Room, once a place of darkness and fear, now became a sanctuary of love and acceptance. And in that sacred space, Pamela and the entity found solace, healing old wounds that had plagued them for so long.

Sex Magick

Pamela's mind was racing as she stood before the strange entity. She had never encountered anything like it before, and yet, here it was, communicating with her telepathically. She couldn't help but feel a sense of awe and wonder at the situation.

"May I inquire as to your name?" Pamela asked tentatively, her thoughts reaching out to the entity.

To her surprise, the entity responded, its voice echoing in her mind. It articulated its name through its contorted and inverted mouth, and Pamela couldn't help but marvel at the sound of it.

"That is an exquisite name!" she exclaimed, her thoughts filled with admiration. "Agnes, did you hear that?"

Agnes, who had been standing nearby, nodded in agreement. "Indeed, I concur," she said. "It is a truly beautiful name."

Pamela couldn't help but feel a sense of connection to the entity, despite its strange appearance. She wondered what other secrets it held, what other mysteries it could reveal to her. For a moment, she felt as though she was on the brink of discovering something truly extraordinary.

The Tower Room itself underwent a notable transformation at this point; the lingering atmosphere of chilling terror was replaced by prevailing vibrations of warm tenderness and a profound connection between Pamela and the creature named Desiree. Furthermore, the room underwent a magnificent transfiguration... This resplendent space, adorned with exquisite architectural marvels, emitted an aura of regality and refinement. The room's majestic structure, meticulously crafted with utmost attention to detail, stood as a testament to the pinnacle of opulence. The women's senses were immediately captivated by the symphony of luxury that enveloped them. The walls, embellished with gilded accents and adorned with intricate tapestries, whispered tales of a bygone era. The ceiling, a masterpiece of artistic prowess, showcased a celestial mural that transported them to a realm of celestial beauty. The room's focal point, a magnificent chandelier, cascaded a shower of shimmering crystals, casting a mesmerizing glow that danced upon the room's sumptuous furnishings. Desiree's contorted form began to vibrate, emitting a low, muffled, humming sound; it appeared to Pamela that the room itself was beginning to hum, gradually commencing a spinning motion. A revelation of a bygone era began to materialize.

Pamela stood transfixed, her eyes fixed upon the mesmerizing marvel before her. The room seemed to fade away as she delved deeper into her thoughts, captivated by the profound revelation that lay before her. The air was thick with anticipation, as if time itself had come to a standstill.

But suddenly, the tranquility was shattered by the intrusion of an ominous figure. A man, with an aura of darkness surrounding him, stepped into the room, his presence framing a look of sheer terror on Pamela's face. It was none other than Aleister Crowley, a name that carried with it a reputation of enigma and malevolence.

As Crowley's piercing gaze met theirs, his lips curled into a sinister smile. His voice, deep and gravelly, broke the silence, sending shivers through the room. "Hello, Agnes," he growled, his words dripping with a venomous tone that echoed in the air.

"I thought you were dead these many years," Agnes retorted, her voice laced with a mixture of surprise and defiance. The words escaped her lips before she could fully grasp the gravity of the situation. Fear and curiosity intertwined within her, as she awaited Crowley's response, unsure of what lay ahead.

"All instances amalgamate into a unified entity - you, being the most knowledgeable, should be well aware of this fact."

"I see that you persist in indulging in your practice of Black Magick; why have you summoned us to reconvene within the initial atmosphere of this chamber?"

"I would like to demonstrate to you the unwavering willpower that still resides within me, as well as to unveil the concealed nature of the small entity among us. It is important to note that she and her lineage represent the enduring consequences of my previous encounter with Lam, which occurred many years ago. She is a Laminite, a direct outcome of the intercourse I shared with them during the practice of Sex Magick.

"In fact, she's not the only one—look about you."

Abruptly, additional diminutive entities manifested themselves, akin to Desiree, as they proceeded to crawl in close proximity to one another.

"It's absolutely grand to have all my children!"

"More akin to woeful and ill-fated progeny birthed from the depths of your malevolent enchantments," snapped Agnes.

"Your words, on the contrary, are lamentable and insufficiently equipped to counteract my intentions for them and the numerous ones that will follow."

"Precisely, what are your intentions regarding them," remarked Pamela.

"You are privileged to witness the birth of a new magical race, conceived through interdimensional intercourse that surpasses the natural order itself."

"Furthermore, may I assert that the aforementioned objectives encompass the desire to triumph over and subjugate the inherent structure of the world? Would it be accurate to state so?" chimed in Agnes.

"Your eloquence with words is truly remarkable, my esteemed former lover. I assure you that my intentions are clear and precise."

As the events unfolded, the diminutive entities, their small figures huddled together in a tight circle, intertwined their hands and connected their minds. A peculiar energy emanated from their collective being, growing in intensity until it transformed into a piercing, shrill sound that reverberated through the air itself.

Caught completely off guard by this unexpected turn of events, Crowley, who had been observing the scene with a mixture of curiosity and trepidation, let out a startled shriek. In an instant, he vanished into thin air, leaving behind nothing but a lingering sense of his presence. As if his disappearance had triggered some sort of mystical mechanism, the Tower Room underwent a swift transformation, reverting back to its original state.

Now, Pamela, Agnes, and Desiree found themselves once again alone in the room, their eyes wide with astonishment and confusion. The air seemed to hold a lingering sense of enchantment, as if the very fabric of reality had been momentarily disrupted by the strange power of the diminutive entities.

Pamela, her heart pounding in her chest, took a hesitant step forward, her gaze darting around the room in search of any clue as to what had just transpired. Agnes, her usually composed demeanor shaken, clutched onto Desiree's arm for support, her mind racing to make sense of the inexplicable events they had just witnessed.

Pamela's voice trembled with anxiety as she struggled to make sense of the bewildering events that had just unfolded before her eyes. She turned to her friend Agnes, hoping for some clarity amidst the chaos.

"I... I am unable to comprehend the sudden manifestation of everything that occurred right in front of me," Pamela confessed, her voice filled with confusion and disbelief. "Agnes, would you kindly elaborate on the events that have just transpired?"

Agnes sighed, her expression reflecting a mix of concern and awe. "Desiree and her siblings have evidently displayed a level of power that surpasses my initial expectations," she explained, her voice tinged with both admiration and apprehension. "Collectively, their psychic capabilities stand unparalleled in terms of their sheer determination. It's truly remarkable."
Pamela's eyes widened, her mind struggling to grasp the magnitude of what Agnes was saying. "But how is that possible?" she asked, her voice filled with genuine curiosity. "How can they possess such extraordinary abilities?"

Agnes paused for a moment, her gaze fixed on the ground as she carefully chose her words. "Aleister," she began, her voice laced with a hint of caution, "lacks any comprehension of the audacious consequences he has recklessly set in motion. His actions have unleashed a force that even he cannot fully comprehend."

Pamela's confusion deepened, her brow furrowing in perplexity. "I find myself perplexed by yet another matter that eludes my comprehension," she admitted, her voice tinged with frustration. "How is it possible that Aleister Crowley remains among the living? I thought he was long gone."

"Aleister's existence defies all logic and reason. It's as if he possesses some sort of immortality, a power that keeps him alive against all odds."

Pamela's mind raced with questions, her curiosity piqued by the enigmatic nature of Aleister's continued presence. "And what about his statement regarding your past romantic involvement?" she asked, her voice filled with anticipation. "What does it mean?"

A Revelation

Agnes replied to Pamela's inquiry, "First and foremost, allow me to state that his ostensible determination was merely superficial. As peculiar as it may sound, I believe that Crowley was genuinely unaware of his own authentic will and spent his entire life chasing a mirage. He was a man of exceptional abilities, often exhibiting brilliance and occasional genius, but he squandered his potential in a juvenile rebellion against authority and a rationalization of every impulse of his insatiable ego. Crowley's life is replete with misfortunes, but this may be the most lamentable of them all. Yet, he has somehow eclipsed time itself.

"However, there was a period during which I was captivated by his charismatic aura and formidable presence. Our relationship evolved into a romantic one, encompassing various forms of intimate encounters. Unbeknownst to me at that time, he was also involved in a romantic relationship with a close friend of mine, Dawn, who also succumbed to his forceful allure. Regrettably, this idyllic situation swiftly transformed into a distressing ordeal. I happened to witness an incident where he violently assaulted Dawn during their participation in one of his Sex Magick circles. Therefore, I present to you my remarkable narrative...

A gathering of indigenous witches, warlocks, and even more sinister entities convened in a dark forest with the purpose of aiding in Dawn's degradation. As she disrobed and approached the feared altar, flanked by unclothed indigenous males donning goat-head masks, I interjected with a fervent plea to Dawn.

"Please, hold on! Do not succumb to their influence. In this very moment, you retain your true identity and possess the liberty to reject their ways and instead embrace righteousness. Dawn, I harbor deep affection for you!"

Dawn slowly emerged from a profound state of detachment and turned to meet my gaze. "What did you just say?" Her eyes widened, now ablaze with a comforting blue glow. How incredibly heartening it was to hear those words.

"I love you, I repeated, my voice filled with urgency. Let's quickly escape from this dreadful place before it's too late!"

In a sudden and terrifying moment, the air was filled with a chilling laughter that seemed to emerge from the depths of hell itself. It was Aleister Crowley, his eyes burning with a fiery intensity, concealed beneath a dark hood. He forcefully positioned himself between myself and Dawn, and without any mercy, he struck me, causing me to collapse to the ground, gasping for air.

Dawn, overwhelmed with fear and concern, instinctively threw herself onto Crowley's back, desperately pleading, "No, Nooo! Please, leave her alone!"

However, Crowley responded with a sinister chuckle, reminiscent of a demonic being, and with a single swift motion, he callously tossed Dawn aside as if she were nothing more than a lifeless rag doll.

Mockingly, Crowley taunted, "Well, well, well... seems like you're losing your courage, Dawn." He continued with a malicious grin, "Well, your dear friend here is about to suffer even more than just a loss of spirit!"

In light of this, Crowley commanded for Dawn to be detained by his repugnant entourage, while she observed with a sense of powerlessness as I was forcibly disrobed, escorted towards the altar, and on the verge of enduring a brutal violation, when a soothing voice broke through the contaminated atmosphere...

A man adorned in a white robe and hood stood upright and confident, firmly gripping a wooden staff in his left hand. "All of you who embody pure hatred and emptiness...I command you, in the name of the spirit that has created all things, to release the young woman!"

Suddenly, the demonic group became feeble and devoid of power. I crawled away from the altar and hurriedly approached Dawn, where we embraced each other in tears. Crowley, refusing to be defeated, summoned his remaining strength and recited an incantation. From the misty air emerged two trees—one beautiful and abundant with fruit, while the other was old and decaying, its branches lifeless.

"Observe," exclaimed Crowley, "that is the 'option' which your acquaintance had mentioned earlier, Dawn. The reality is, my dear that you are left with no alternative but to SELECT one of them at present. One presents the prospect of eternal beauty, while the other only guarantees wretchedness, deterioration, and demise!!!"

The two young women remained trembling as I endeavored to approach the hooded figure who had just preserved my honor and existence.

"Kind sir, I implore you...please...please assure us that his words are false—aid us in escaping this location!" I pleaded, my voice filled with tears.

"I am afraid that he is speaking the truth... I do not possess any authority over this matter. As it was in the past, so it shall be now and in the future. The task must be accomplished; your friend must make this decision independently, without any intervention," stated the timely visitor dressed in white.

Dawn's senses became numbed as she observed me, as I wept, attentively observing the transformation of my friend's expression from fear and horror to a perplexed frown. Subsequently, a smile gradually emerged on Dawn's countenance, accompanied by a soft laughter that escalated in volume.

"How foolish of me to have momentarily succumbed to weakness," Dawn uttered. "Of course, I am aware of which option to select... Just imagine, Agnes, I will acquire boundless knowledge, never again experiencing powerlessness, and above all else—I will forever remain youthful!"

"DAWN!!! No! Refrain from approaching that tree!!!" I implored, rushing towards my companion.

The White visitor urgently addressed me, attempting to prevent myself from taking action. However, it was too late. Dawn forcefully pushed me aside, causing me to stumble into The Other Tree and become impaled by its sharp thorns.

"Agnes, it was unwise of you to attempt to impede me. Your appearance is pitiable and foolish. Did you truly believe that I would choose something as grotesque as that over the feast that I am about to partake in?" Dawn's words were spoken in a tone of condescension and disdain.

Bleeding from the thorns that had torn my skin, I watched in agony as Dawn approached the bountiful tree and indulged in its offerings. Once she had satisfied her hunger, Dawn caressed the tree's soft bark, unaware that its branches were slowly descending upon her. A piercing scream escaped her lips as she was ensnared by the tree's vice-like grip. Crowley, observing from a distance, chuckled to himself in a macabre manner as he witnessed a large, black serpent descend from the tree's canopy and coil itself around Dawn, its target. After emerging from Dawn, the serpent vanished in a blaze of fire, leaving me in tears. My sorrowful appearance provoked an insatiable fury within Crowley, who proceeded to charge towards me with the intention of forcibly extracting me from The Other Tree and claiming me as his own. However, a surrounding mist of a "blue" hue impeded his progress, causing him to express his disdain through a hiss. He then proceeded to retrieve the unconscious body of Dawn, hoisting her over his shoulder before vanishing into the encroaching darkness, accompanied by his mischievous accomplices who limped after him.

Upon the dispersion of the malevolent group, I gradually succumbed to unconsciousness while the enigmatic individual, cloaked in white, delicately lowered my body from The Other Tree. Gradually regaining my strength, I raised my gaze as the white figure suddenly doubled over in apparent agony, revealing a silver medallion protruding from beneath the hooded garment. I hurried to his side, intending to offer assistance, yet he shook his head ever so gently, his breath labored, and slowly elevated himself onto his knees, beginning to remove his hood. I was horrified by the sight of an exceedingly elderly man, struggling for breath and possessing a voice that resembled the sound of impending demise.

He uttered, "My time is rapidly drawing to a close... I have fulfilled my journey and purpose... now it is time for your mission to commence..."

He rose gradually, removed his white cowl, and draped it over my unclothed form. Despite the malodorous emanations from his emaciated physique, he endeavored to suppress any wheezing as I observed with complete astonishment. He then proceeded to remove the silver medallion from around his neck and placed it upon my own before drawing the white hood over my serene countenance.

"Pursue The Order of The Other Side...the medallion shall serve as an indication to them that your Time has come...it...It is finished!"

I was captivated as the ground trembled and the Great Other Tree emerged from the soil, its opulent roots creeping towards the corpse of the deceased elderly gentleman, enveloping him in a shroud-like tissue before receding back into the earth. Subsequently, the Other Tree gradually dissipated.

I once had an alliance with the Jesuit Order of Priests. They were completely unaware of my enigmatic man dressed in white, had no knowledge of the existence of the Order of The Other Side, and even went as far as threatening me with Ex-Communication unless I repented for my fantastical account and engaged in "intensive" spiritual guidance to purify my soul from an excessive imagination. The Vicar General believed that I required an exorcism, but rather than subject myself to this potentially oppressive religious constraint, I decided to embark on a voyage to Europe, enduring a long and arduous journey in the hopes of uncovering any trace of this enigmatic "Order".

Following numerous encounters with clandestine organizations in the heart of Slavic territories, my expedition culminated in the rugged, mountainous terrain of Tibet. In this remote location, free from the corrupting influences of the West, I discovered a small community of hermits consisting of both Asian and Caucasian men and women. These individuals exchanged knowledge and insight within cells hewn into the rock, and were collectively known as The Order of The Other Side. Upon revealing my "medallion", I was warmly received as a novice into their community.

After dedicating eight years to extensive prayer, study, and a rigorous discipline of dervish dances, I acquired a wealth of Wisdom and attained the fruits of Contemplation, thus preparing myself for final vows. However, prior to taking this significant step, I was guided into the chamber of the esteemed Grand Master in the Art of Unknowing, Meister Ciparis. It was there that I discovered the truth regarding my encounter with the Old Man in White, who had saved my life on that unforgettable evening. This mysterious figure turned out to be a former Carthusian Monk who had departed from his Order in late 13th century France, an act commonly referred to as "jumping the wall." His journey eventually led him to The Order of the Other Side, a clandestine and ancient community deeply immersed in enigmatic practices. Within this order, he was initiated into the High Art of Unknowing, which involved comprehending the path that leads to the ultimate questions and answers of all that exists. To embark upon this journey, one must first "UNKNOW" everything, as the source behind all things cannot be fully comprehended or grasped. By embracing this "Way," a protective Cloud of Unknowing descends upon the individual, rendering any malevolent forces dormant in its presence.

Evil endeavors to dominate and exert control over all that is known, yet the Source of all creation possesses an enigmatic nature that renders evil bewildered and powerless in the Presence of the Good. The aforementioned individual, a former Carthusian, was among the "chosen" few whose Love burned so fervently for this Unknown Wisdom that a transformation occurred, one that bears the Mark of the Great Other Tree. Receiving this gift entails a consequential responsibility, as one is ordained to traverse the earth on a mission to liberate those whose lives are held captive by the forces of darkness. This wandering shall not cease until the last "branch" appears on the Silver Medallion of the Great Other Tree. Until such a moment arrives, however, a branch will continue to sprout on the medallion, a result of someone being lifted from the shackles of enslaving shadows. This benevolent man, who still donned his White Carthusian habit and the medallion around his neck, roamed for centuries, freeing hapless victims from the curse of darkness, with myself being his last and ultimate encounter.

"My Dear Pamela, I have hereby presented to you my peculiar narrative. I have undertaken my itinerant quest with valor and resilience, with the intention of one day emancipating Dawn from the vile clutches of Aleister Crowley. However, upon my return after a prolonged twelve-year absence, I was disheartened to learn that she had already departed and was nowhere to be found."

The Six Towers

Self-gnosis

In the presence of Agnes, Pamela couldn't help but feel a deep admiration for the woman's narrative. Agnes' remarkable courage and unwavering dedication to her chosen path left Pamela in awe. She couldn't help but express her admiration, addressing Agnes in a sincere and heartfelt manner.

"I deeply admire your remarkable courage and unwavering dedication to the path that lies ahead of you, Agnes," Pamela said, her voice filled with genuine admiration. "Your journey has inspired me in ways I cannot fully explain. It's as if our encounter was destined to occur, allowing me to derive inspiration from your exceptional spiritual fortitude."

Pamela's words hung in the air, the weight of her admiration palpable. She couldn't help but wonder how she could embark on a similar path, how she could find the same sense of purpose and strength that Agnes possessed. With a mix of curiosity and determination, she turned to Agnes, seeking guidance.

"Curiously, I find myself inexplicably drawn towards the same direction," Pamela confessed. "It's as if something within me resonates with the path you have chosen. I feel a deep longing to embark on a similar journey, to find the same sense of purpose and fulfillment. What steps must I take to initiate this request?"

Agnes listened attentively, her eyes filled with understanding. She knew the yearning Pamela felt, the desire to embark on a transformative journey. With a calm and reassuring voice, she responded.

"If one is earnest, it is indeed necessary to undertake the prescribed measures," Agnes explained. "The solution to your personal request lies within the six pillars of discernment."

As Agnes spoke, Pamela felt a strange sensation coursing through her body. It was as if something deep within her was calling out, beckoning her to come closer. She couldn't quite put her finger on it, but she knew that she had to follow this feeling, to explore the path that Agnes had embarked upon.

She was suddenly transported to a deep forest, and as the trees began to thin out, she found herself standing in a clearing. It was then that she saw it - a vision of Six Towers began to enfold before her countenance.

Pamela couldn't resist the allure of the towers and took hesitant steps towards them. As she approached, the air around her seemed to change, becoming charged with an otherworldly energy.

The closer she got, the more she noticed the intricate details of the towers. Each one had a unique design, with delicate carvings and ornate balconies. The sunlight danced off the golden surface, casting a warm glow that enveloped the clearing.

With each step, Pamela felt a strange connection to the towers. It was as if they held a secret, a hidden knowledge that only she could uncover. The air whispered ancient tales, and she could almost hear the echoes of forgotten voices.

Abruptly, she perceived the sound of Agnes' vocalization.

"Behold the magnificent spectacle that unfolds before your very eyes - a collection of six resplendent towers, each one shrouded in an enigmatic allure that beckons you to embark on a journey of discovery. As you traverse from one tower to the next, prepare to unlock the hidden treasures concealed within their walls, for only the most astute minds shall unravel their mysteries."

Without hesitation, Pamela began to walk towards the towers. As she got closer, she could see that each tower had a different symbol etched into the wall. One had a sun, another a moon, and another a star.

As she reached out to touch the wall of the tower with the moon symbol, she felt a surge of energy flow through her body. It was as if the tower was alive, and it was communicating with her in a language that she couldn't quite understand.

As the towering doors of the magnificent structure swung open, Pamela stepped forward, her heart pounding with anticipation. The grandeur of the first tower enveloped her, its opulence evident in every intricate detail. The air was thick with an aura of mystery, as if the very walls whispered secrets only the chosen few were privy to.

At that moment there appeared a primordial being which spoke thusly to Pamela:

"I am but one of the enigmatic dark messengers, entrusted with the sacred duty of guarding the threshold. Within the confines of our towering abodes, we diligently delve into the depths of ancient knowledge, seeking to unravel the enigmatic dark gnosis that lies hidden within the fabric of existence. It is our solemn purpose to bring forth this profound wisdom, meticulously transcribing it onto a scroll, so that it may be unveiled to those who seek its elusive truths.

"In the ethereal realm where we reside, time seems to lose its grip, as we immerse ourselves in the timeless pursuit of understanding the mysteries that shroud our world. Each of us, in our respective towers, is consumed by an insatiable hunger for knowledge, driven by an unyielding desire to decipher the cryptic messages that have been bestowed upon us.

"As the moon casts its pale glow upon the ancient manuscripts that adorn our chambers, we embark on a journey of enlightenment. With quill in hand and inkwell at the ready, we meticulously transcribe the profound revelations that have been unveiled to us. The delicate strokes of our pens dance across the parchment, etching the sacred symbols and intricate patterns that hold the key to unlocking the secrets of the universe.

"The dark gnosis, like a veil of shadows, conceals itself within the recesses of our minds. It is a clandestine force that beckons us, urging us to delve deeper into the abyss of knowledge. We tread cautiously, for the path we traverse is treacherous, fraught with the perils of madness and enlightenment. Yet, undeterred by the dangers that lie ahead, we persist, driven by an unwavering determination to bring forth the wisdom that has been entrusted to us.

"And so, as the moon wanes and the stars align, we complete our sacred task. The scroll, adorned with intricate symbols and imbued with the essence of the dark gnosis, is ready to be unveiled. It is a vessel of enlightenment, a conduit through which the elusive truths of the universe shall be revealed to those who dare to seek them.

"With reverence and anticipation, we present this scroll to you, dear seeker of knowledge. May its contents illuminate your path, guiding you through the labyrinthine corridors of existence. Embrace the wisdom it imparts, for within its ancient script lies the power to transcend the boundaries of mortal understanding."

As Pamela's trembling fingers reached out to touch the scroll, a surge of energy coursed through her. Suddenly, the parchment began to unfurl itself, as if guided by an unseen force. Pamela's mind's eye was captivated, her senses heightened, as the words and images on the scroll danced before her.

In that moment, she felt a connection to something far greater than herself. The scroll revealed secrets and knowledge that had been hidden for centuries, a tapestry of wisdom woven by the hands of those who came before her. It was as if the very essence of the tower had been captured within those ancient writings.

Pamela's heart raced with excitement and curiosity, her mind ablaze with questions. What did these words hold? What truths would be unveiled? With each passing moment, she felt herself being drawn deeper into the labyrinth of knowledge, her thirst for understanding growing stronger.

As the scroll continued to unfold, Pamela took a deep breath, ready to embrace the mysteries as the delicate parchment gracefully unfurled—a mesmerizing revelation began to unfold, unveiling the profound secrets that lay within.

In the pursuit of Self-gnosis, there comes a profound realization that transcends any notion of triumph or jubilation. Instead, it is a moment of awakening to the stark truth that we, as mere mortals, hold no dominion over the intricate workings of our own fragmented body-consciousness. It is a humbling experience, one that demands us to acknowledge the stark reality that our lives remain bereft of the all-encompassing radiance emanating from the Nirvanic Element of truth.

In this journey towards Self-gnosis, we embark upon a path of self-discovery that unravels the layers of our existence, peeling back the veils of illusion that shroud our perception. As we delve deeper into the recesses of our being, we come face to face with the limitations of our mortal selves, realizing that our control over the intricate tapestry of our lives is but an illusion.

No longer can we cling to the false sense of power and authority we once believed we possessed. The moment of Self-gnosis strips away these illusions, leaving us vulnerable and exposed to the raw truth of our insignificance in the grand scheme of existence. It is a moment that demands humility, as we confront the undeniable truth that we are but tiny specks in the vast cosmic web.

Gone are the illusions of grandeur and the false narratives we constructed to shield ourselves from the harsh realities of life. In the light of Self-gnosis, we are forced to confront the stark emptiness that pervades our lives, the absence of the undivided light that illuminates the path to ultimate truth. It is a moment of reckoning, where we must confront the void within ourselves and acknowledge our desperate need for the Nirvanic Element to fill the void.

Yet, amidst the humbling realization of our mortal limitations, there lies a glimmer of hope. For in acknowledging our powerlessness, we open ourselves to the possibility of growth and transformation. The moment of Self-gnosis becomes a catalyst for change, a stepping stone towards a deeper understanding of our place in the universe.

As we embrace our humility, we begin to recognize the interconnectedness of all beings, the intricate threads that bind us together in this vast cosmic tapestry. We realize that our journey towards Self-gnosis is not a solitary one, but a collective endeavor shared by all who seek truth and enlightenment. And so, in this extended narrative of Self-gnosis, we find ourselves at the crossroads of humility and hope.

As Pamela stood there, a sudden and overwhelming sense of freedom washed over her. It was a feeling she had never experienced before, and it was as if a weight had been lifted from her shoulders. For the first time in her life, she felt truly liberated.

Gone were the chains that had bound her to her ego, and she was no longer trapped in the endless cycle of suffering and desire. She was free to be who she truly was, without any fear or hesitation. It was as if a veil had been lifted from her eyes, and she could finally see the world in all its beauty and wonder.

Pamela realized that she was no longer just a mere mortal, but a vessel for the divine. She was a part of something much greater than herself, and she felt a deep sense of purpose and meaning in her life. She knew that she had been given a gift, and she was determined to use it to make a difference in the world.

Pamela felt a sense of awe and wonder. She knew that there was so much more to life than what she had previously thought, and she was excited to explore all the possibilities that lay ahead. With a newfound sense of freedom and purpose, she set out on a journey to the Second Tower filled with self-discovery and enlightenment, ready to embrace all that would be revealed.

Recollective Resolve

Deep within the confines of the Second Tower, where only those who have embarked on the path of enlightenment are permitted to reside, the inhabitants are acutely aware of the immense power of Recollective Resolve. This unyielding determination is absolutely essential for them to persevere through the grueling journey towards spiritual awakening. They comprehend that without this unwavering resolve, they may be easily swayed by the alluring temptations that lurk around every corner, threatening to derail their progress and plunge them back into the abyss of their former miserable states of mind.

The inhabitants of the Second Tower have learned through experience that the path to enlightenment is not an easy one. It is fraught with obstacles and challenges that test their resolve at every turn. They know that the journey requires a steadfast commitment to their goals and an unshakeable determination to overcome any obstacles that may arise. They understand that the only way to achieve true spiritual awakening is to remain focused and determined, even in the face of adversity.

The potency of Recollective Resolve is not lost on these enlightened individuals. They have witnessed firsthand the transformative power of this unwavering determination. They know that it is the key to unlocking the full potential of their minds and souls. With Recollective Resolve as their guiding light, they are able to navigate the treacherous waters of the spiritual journey with confidence and grace.

In the chambers of the Second Tower, the inhabitants live and breathe Recollective Resolve. It is the foundation upon which their entire existence is built. They know that without it, they would be lost in the darkness, unable to find their way back to the light. But with it, they are able to transcend their former selves and reach new heights of spiritual enlightenment.

Despite being aware of the potential consequences, the allure of abandoning their progress and surrendering to their miserable states of mind was a constant presence for them. The familiar and comforting nature of their past experiences called out to them like a captivating melody, tempting them to give in.

After reading the scroll, Pamela found herself entangled in an internal struggle. She had made significant advancements in her journey, yet the weight of her past hardships and the fear of the unknown still haunted her. She felt adrift, as if she were lost in a vast sea of uncertainty, with no one to guide her.

As Pamela ventured into the depths of the Second Tower, a sense of trepidation gripped her heart. The weight of her battle seemed to grow heavier with each step she took, threatening to crush her spirit. But little did she know, she was not destined to face this daunting journey alone.

Pamela found herself surrounded by a group of individuals, their comforting presence enveloping her like a warm embrace. One of them, with a voice so tender and soothing, spoke up, breaking the silence that had weighed heavily upon her. "You are not alone, Pamela," he reassured her, his words carrying a profound sense of understanding. "We have all experienced the very same struggles that you are facing right now.
However, we have discovered a remarkable companion in our journey called the Recollective Resolve. It possesses an extraordinary power, capable of aiding us in conquering any obstacle that may appear insurmountable."

In that moment, Pamela felt a glimmer of hope ignite within her. The weight of her burdens seemed to lessen as she absorbed the wisdom shared by these compassionate souls. She realized that she was not the only one who had traversed this treacherous path, and that there were others who had emerged triumphant on the other side.

Curiosity sparked within her, and she couldn't help but inquire further. "How does this Recollective Resolve work?" she asked, her voice filled with both eagerness and a hint of skepticism.

A gentle smile graced the face of the person who had spoken earlier, his eyes radiating warmth and empathy.

"The Recollective Resolve," he began, "is a formidable force that resides within each and every one of us. It is a reservoir of strength, resilience, and unwavering determination. When we tap into it, we unlock a wellspring of potential that empowers us to overcome even the most daunting of challenges."

Pamela's curiosity deepened, her skepticism slowly giving way to a glimmer of belief. She yearned to understand how this intangible ally could truly make a difference in her life.

"It begins," the person continued, "by acknowledging that the obstacles we face are not insurmountable mountains, but rather stepping stones on our path to growth and self-discovery. The Recollective Resolve helps us shift our perspective, enabling us to see these obstacles as opportunities for personal transformation."

As the words resonated within Pamela's heart, she felt a flicker of courage ignite within her. The notion that her struggles were not roadblocks, but rather catalysts for her own evolution, filled her with a newfound sense of purpose.

With her determination reignited, she redirected her focus back to her contemplation, prepared to confront any challenges that lay ahead. She knew that she would not be alone in her endeavors, for the spiritual companions of the Second Tower would be there to support her every step of the way. With the Recollective Resolve as her guiding light, she was confident that she would emerge from this journey stronger and wiser, ready to face whatever the future held.

Purgation

As Pamela stepped through the towering entrance of The Third Tower, a mysterious voice resonated through the air, reaching her ears with an ethereal presence. "There is no security in this life," the voice, ancient and primordial, declared, its words carrying a weight of wisdom. It seemed to echo from the depths of time itself, as if spoken by the very essence of existence.

Caught off guard by the unexpected greeting, Pamela's curiosity was piqued. She couldn't help but wonder about the meaning behind those profound words. What did it truly mean to have no security in life? Was it a warning, a reminder of the ever-changing nature of the world? Or perhaps it was an invitation to embrace the unknown, to let go of the illusion of control and find solace in the unpredictability of existence.

As these thoughts swirled in her mind, the voice continued, its tone both soothing and commanding. "We must learn to embrace the uncertainty," it urged, as if imparting a timeless lesson. Pamela felt a sense of intrigue and anticipation building within her, as if she was about to embark on a deeper profound journey of self-discovery.

"And to find strength in our spirit," the voice concluded, its words resonating deep within Pamela's being. It was a call to tap into the inner reservoirs of resilience and courage, to draw upon the untapped potential that lay dormant within her soul. The voice seemed to imply that true strength was not found in external circumstances or material possessions, but rather in the depths of one's own spirit.

Pamela stood there, in the grandeur of the Third Tower, feeling a newfound sense of purpose and determination. She realized that this encounter was no mere coincidence, but a pivotal moment in her life's journey. With each step she took, she vowed to embrace the uncertainty that lay ahead, to face the challenges with unwavering strength, and to discover the depths of her own spirit.

And so, Pamela ventured forth into the Third Tower, her heart filled with anticipation and her mind open to the infinite possibilities that awaited her. Little did she know that this encounter with the enigmatic voice would shape her destiny, leading her towards a path of self-discovery, resilience, and a profound understanding of the true nature of security in this ever-changing world. Again, she looked to the scroll.

Do not allow your aversions to consume you. Whenever we experience aversions in life, they only become worse when we react to them in a negative manner. Instead of immediately labeling them as oppressors, take a step back and evaluate them in the perspective of the Unborn, which always exposes the self-oppressive nature of our ego. It is true, we hold onto our false sense of self too dearly! Moreover, self-importance is the main culprit behind all of this; it is like a demon! It stands in direct opposition to Self-Realization, which is achieved through self-awareness and understanding that these flaws in life are inherently empty and lack any true substance. They can be compared to two ghostly ships passing each other on a foggy night, both lacking true substance and destined to fade away. Above all, strive to respond to any situation with compassion.

In the realm of absolute assurance, there lies a profound understanding that every obstacle and challenge can be conquered. It is an unwavering recognition that the tumultuous nature of samsara, the cycle of birth and death, holds no inherent reality within itself. It is akin to the suffering experienced in a dream, an illusion that lacks substance in the waking world.

Moreover, this realization unveils the presence of negative karma, the consequences of past actions, manifesting in the form of adversity. It is an ugly head that rears itself, reminding us of the consequences of our past deeds. However, within this recognition lies a precious opportunity, a chance to transform this negative karma into a positive force.

To let this opportunity slip through our fingers would be a grave mistake, for the repercussions of negative karma will undoubtedly follow us into future lives. Therefore, it becomes imperative to seize this moment and redirect the energy of negativity towards a positive path. This can be achieved through the accumulation of good merit, engaging in virtuous actions that bring about positive consequences.

Additionally, seeking the assistance of Divine Agencies becomes crucial in this pivotal transformation of negative energy. By invoking their guidance and support, we can navigate through the challenges and obstacles that lie ahead. They become our allies in this journey of turning the tides and cultivating positive reinforcement.

As Pamela delved deeper into her spiritual journey, she came to a profound realization - it was a path of purgation that lay before her. This path served as a metaphor, symbolizing the need to shed all worldly attachments and desires in order to gain a clearer understanding of the necessity for renunciation and, subsequently, purgation of the limitations imposed by the physical and mental aspects of existence. Only then could the soul break free from its confinements and soar to the lofty heights of the Unborn.

However, Pamela understood that this process of purgation was not an easy one. It required traversing the stage of spiritual adolescence, a crucial phase that could not be bypassed. Failing to navigate this stage would result in a dreadful spiritual dryness that would persist indefinitely. The flow of spiritual energy, like a vital juice, needed to be unimpeded, but first, one had to set aside the ego-driven tendencies of childishness. Often, individuals would abandon their spiritual journey altogether, opting to retreat to the familiar and unremarkable harbor of mediocrity.

Purgation, Pamela realized, came at a cost. This cost could manifest in various forms - financial burdens or the arduous task of overcoming persistent physical and mental challenges. Renunciation, she understood, could not be achieved without first engaging in the Recollective-Resolve, a deep commitment to the path, and attaining meditative-equipoise, a state of inner balance and tranquility. It was only when the True-Spiritual Sojourner, the dedicated practitioner, achieved a state of ecstatic union with the Unborn Lord and performed all actions solely for the Self-Supreme that the remnants of past karmic influences were obliterated in the eternal flame of pure intellect.

Triumphing over the limitations of the body-consciousness, while simultaneously fulfilling the basic needs of the physical form, sojourners carry out one's sacred actions not as mere mortal agents but as embodiments of the Self-Supreme, permeating the surrounding world with divine essence.

Quietude

As Pamela continued on her journey, she eventually found herself standing at the very heart of the Fourth Tower. This particular Tower was dedicated to the practice of meditation, specifically the meditation of Recollection and its subsequent outcome: the Contemplation of Quietude. This was a highly significant practice, one that was said to bring about a multitude of effects.

The wise and experienced practitioner, describes the meditation of Recollection as a supernatural experience, one that was distinct from simply closing one's eyes or being in darkness. It was a state of mind that did not rely on any external factors, but rather occurred naturally, without any deliberate intention. It was as if the very act of closing one's eyes and seeking solitude was enough to lay the foundation for this powerful meditation.

As Pamela began to practice this meditation, she felt the grip of her senses and external distractions slowly begin to loosen. It was as if her soul was reclaiming something that it had previously lost. The distractions of the outside world began to fade away, leaving her with a sense of peace and tranquility that she had never experienced before. It was a truly transformative experience, one that would surely stay with her for the rest of her life.

The subsequent section of the scroll predominantly conveyed a parable:

Once upon a time, in a far-off land, there lived a great King who resided in the center of a magnificent castle. He was a kind and merciful ruler who always looked after his people. One day, as he was surveying his kingdom, he noticed that some of his subjects had strayed away from their dwelling place and were lost in the wilderness. Despite their disobedience, the King saw their good will and desired to bring them back to himself.

Like a good shepherd, the King used a whistle so gentle that even the lost subjects almost failed to hear it. However, the whistle had such power that it made them recognize the King's voice and stopped them from going further astray. The lost subjects were drawn back to their dwelling place by the gentle sound of the King's whistle.

The wise of the kingdom spoke of hearing about this supernal whistle. It was likened to Parato ghosa, a great deathless sound that is not heard in the conventional sense of hearing. Rather, it is a sublime "inward self-realization" that can only be discerned within one's own inner-spiritual Ear.

When one hears the wonderful voice of the Sugata, they are actually being filled with the compassionate and primordial wisdom that reflects the inner sacred sound of suchness (tathata) itself. It is a soundless sound that can only be felt within one's being.

Although it is unclear how the lost subjects heard the King's whistle, it was not through their ears. Instead, they noticed a gentle drawing inward, like a hedgehog curling up or a turtle drawing into a shell. This inward drawing was a sign that they were being called back to their dwelling place by the King's gentle whistle.

The King's whistle was a symbol of his compassion and mercy towards his subjects. It showed that he was willing to forgive their disobedience and bring them back to the safety of their homes. The lost subjects were grateful for the King's kindness and were filled with a sense of belonging as they returned to their dwelling place.

In conclusion, the story of the King and his lost subjects is a beautiful metaphor for the compassionate and merciful nature of a great ruler. It also speaks to the power of the inner self-realization that can only be felt within one's being. The King's whistle was a reminder that even in the darkest of times, there is always a way back to the safety of home.

Everything in this journey depends on the Contemplation of Quietude, a state of deep introspection that soothes the restless soul and allows it to connect with its Unborn-Self. In this state, the soul becomes one with the tranquility and calmness it discovers in the "repose of contemplation". This comes after exhausting all previous forms of meditation and finally finding solace in the exclusive focus on the Divine Itself. Essentially, the Contemplation of Quietude is about delving deep within oneself, free from any external disturbances, and finding solace in the serene peace and quiet that embodies the Absolute Nature of the Unborn. It is in this state that one discovers spiritual repose and eternal delight.

Pamela's journey of self-discovery took a profound turn as she experienced a newfound sense of enlightenment. It was as if a veil had been lifted, revealing a deeper understanding of herself and her place in the world. The Contemplation of Quietude, a sacred practice bestowed upon her, had unlocked a wellspring of spiritual consolations and growth within her.

No longer did Pamela have to rely only on external forces or seek solace in various meditations to nurture her spiritual well-being. The Contemplation of Quietude had become her guiding light, illuminating the path towards inner peace and personal growth. It was a gift that transcended the limitations of the physical world, allowing her to tap into a well of wisdom and tranquility that resided within her own being.

With this newfound realization, Pamela felt a profound sense of liberation. She no longer felt the need to seek validation or fulfillment from external sources. Instead, she embraced the power within herself to cultivate her own spiritual journey. The Contemplation of Quietude had become her constant companion, offering solace and guidance whenever she needed it.

As Pamela delved deeper into the practice, she discovered that the Contemplation of Quietude was not just a means to find temporary solace or fleeting moments of enlightenment. It was a transformative force that propelled her towards spiritual growth and self-realization. Through this practice, she began to unravel the layers of her own consciousness, peeling back the barriers that had hindered her from fully embracing her true potential.

Gone were the days of seeking external validation or relying on outside agencies for spiritual nourishment. Pamela had found a wellspring of strength and wisdom within herself, a source that would never run dry. The Contemplation of Quietude had become her anchor, grounding her in times of uncertainty and guiding her towards a deeper understanding of her own spirituality.

With each passing day, Pamela's spiritual journey continued to unfold, revealing new insights and revelations. She marveled at the profound impact the Contemplation of Quietude had on her life, forever altering her perspective and transforming her into a more enlightened and self-assured individual.

In the end, Pamela realized that true spiritual growth and self-realization could only be achieved from within. The Contemplation of Quietude had gifted her with the tools to embark further on this transformative journey, empowering her to find solace, wisdom, and growth in the depths of her own being. From that moment forward, she knew that she would never have to depend on external agencies or meditations.

The Silkworm

Pamela slowly opened her eyes, feeling groggy and disoriented. She blinked a few times, trying to adjust to the dim light of the room. As she sat up, she realized that something was very wrong. Her body felt strange, as if it had been stretched and elongated. She looked down at herself and gasped in horror.

Where her arms and legs had been, there were now six long, slender appendages. Her skin was covered in soft, silky fur, and she had a pair of large, black eyes on either side of her head. She was a giant silkworm.

Pamela couldn't believe what had happened to her. She had been so excited to spend the night in the Fifth Tower, but now she was trapped in this bizarre form. She tried to move, but her new body was awkward and unfamiliar. She felt a surge of panic rising in her chest.

As she looked around the room, she noticed that everything seemed different. The furniture was huge, towering over her tiny form. The windows were high up on the wall, and she could barely see out of them. She realized that she was in a completely different world, one where she was no longer human.

Pamela knew that she had to find a way to reverse the transformation. She had to get back to her own body, her own life. But how? She had no idea how this had happened, or how to undo it. All she could do was wait and hope that someone would come to her rescue.

As the hours passed, Pamela grew more and more anxious. She tried to eat some of the leaves that were scattered around the room, but they tasted strange and unfamiliar. She curled up in a corner, feeling helpless and alone.

Finally, as the sun began to set, she heard a faint scratching at the door. She crawled over to investigate, using her new legs to propel herself forward. As she reached the door, it swung open, revealing a figure standing in the doorway.

It was one of the Primordial-Guardians of the threshold, dressed in a long robe and carrying a staff. He looked down at Pamela with a mixture of surprise and amusement.

"Well, well," he said. "What have we here? A little silkworm, all alone in the tower. How did you get here, my dear?"

Pamela tried to speak, but all that came out was a soft, rustling sound. The Primordial chuckled.

"Don't worry, little one," he said. "I can help you."

As the Primordial gazed down upon Pamela's newly transformed body, now resembling a delicate silkworm, he blinked his eyes in contemplation. With a gentle voice, he spoke, "Do not be disconcerted by your current predicament, for within it lies a wondrous opportunity for a profound spiritual metamorphosis."

Pamela, bewildered by her altered form, looked up at the Primordial with a mixture of curiosity and apprehension as his words both intrigued and perplexed her. How could she possibly spin a cocoon around herself? And what kind of transformation awaited her within?

The Primordial, sensing her uncertainty, extended a reassuring hand towards Pamela. "Fear not, dear one," he said, his voice carrying a soothing warmth. "Within the confines of your self-woven cocoon, you shall embark upon a journey of profound self-discovery and growth. Just as a caterpillar undergoes a remarkable transformation within its chrysalis, so too shall you experience a metamorphosis of the spirit."

Pamela's initial trepidation began to give way to a glimmer of excitement. The Primordial's words resonated deep within her, stirring a dormant sense of adventure and curiosity. She had always yearned for something more, a deeper understanding of herself and the world around her. Perhaps this unexpected transformation held the key to unlocking those hidden truths.

With newfound determination, Pamela nodded, accepting the Primordial's guidance. She closed her eyes, allowing her mind to focus on the task at hand. Imagining herself encased within a cocoon, she visualized the delicate threads weaving together, forming a protective sanctuary around her.

As Pamela immersed herself in this mental cocoon, a profound stillness enveloped her being. Time seemed to stand still, and she felt a profound connection to the very essence of her existence. In this suspended state, she could sense the energy of transformation coursing through her veins, awakening dormant potentials and shedding old limitations.

Days turned into weeks in the Fifth Tower, and Pamela remained steadfast within her self-woven cocoon. She could feel the subtle shifts occurring within her, as if her very essence was being refined and purified. The Primordial, ever watchful, observed her progress with a sense of quiet satisfaction. He knew that within this transformative process, Pamela was undergoing a profound spiritual rebirth.

As she lay there, wrapped tightly in her cocoon, she could feel the anticipation building within her. She knew that something incredible was about to happen, something that would change her forever. And then, with a sudden surge of energy, she began to emerge from her cocoon.

At first, it was a slow and gentle process. She carefully pushed her way out of the tight confines of her cocoon, feeling the soft, silky threads sliding against her skin. As she emerged further and further, she could feel a sense of transformation taking place within her. It was as if she was shedding her old self and becoming something entirely new.

Finally, with a burst of energy, she broke free from her cocoon and stood before the world as a transformed being. She felt almost angelic, with a sense of lightness and grace that she had never experienced before. It was as if she had been reborn, and she wanted nothing more than to spread her wings and soar.

With this new and vitalizing self-realization, she knew that she could accomplish anything she set her mind to. She was no longer bound by the limitations of her old self, but was free to explore the ways of the Spirit and all its possibilities.

As she stood before the Primordial, she felt a sense of awe and reverence wash over her. The ancient being smiled at her, his eyes twinkling with a deep wisdom that seemed to span eons. "This newfound Illumination," he said, his voice resonating with a power that seemed to come from beyond this world, "in the spiritual sense means 'turning on the Light' of the Deathless Unborn Mind. It is a preparation for the spiritual union to the Unborn Lord, which will take place in the Sixth Tower.

"Your newfound Natural State, my dear friend, is none other than the pure essence of the Nature of the Unborn Mind. It is a state of being that can be attained effortlessly, without the need for any specific focus or meditation technique. In fact, it is in the absence of such deliberate efforts that one truly discovers and embraces this profound state.

"Imagine, if you will, a state of mind where you are not fixated on any particular object or thought. A state where your consciousness is not directed towards any specific aim or purpose. It is in this state of non-focus, this state of simply being, that you will come to realize the true essence of the Natural State, something you will come to know eventually in your spiritual progress as the Dharmakaya.

"This Nature, my friend, is not bound by the constraints of time or circumstance. It does not ebb and flow like the tides of the ocean or the passing of seasons. It is a constant presence, always with you, waiting to be recognized and embraced.

"If you can truly believe that this Nature is the very essence of the Natural State, then you will come to understand that there is no need for any particular method or technique of meditation. There is no need to manipulate or alter your state of mind in any way. Simply let it be, as it is, and allow yourself to be enveloped by the profound simplicity and beauty of the Dharmakaya.

"So, my dear friend, let go of any preconceived notions or expectations. Release the need to strive or struggle. Instead, surrender to the inherent wisdom and tranquility of the Natural State. In doing so, you will discover a profound sense of peace and harmony that transcends the limitations of the ordinary mind."

Pamela sat in awe as she contemplated her newfound self-discovery. She couldn't help but wonder what the phrase "Union with the Unborn Lord in the Sixth Tower" truly meant. Her mind raced with questions and possibilities, and she couldn't shake the feeling that this was a pivotal moment in her life.

As she sat there, lost in thought, she couldn't help but reflect on the journey that had led her to this point. It had been a long and winding road, full of twists and turns, but she had finally arrived at a place of clarity and understanding.
Pamela had always been a seeker, someone who was constantly searching for meaning and purpose in her life. She had explored countless spiritual practices and philosophies, but nothing had ever quite resonated with her in the way that this new discovery had.

The phrase "Union with the Unborn Lord in the Sixth Tower" had come to her in a moment of deep meditation, and it had felt like a bolt of lightning striking her soul. She had felt a profound sense of connection and belonging, as if she had finally found the missing piece of the puzzle that had been eluding her for so long.

Now, as she sat there, contemplating what this new path might entail, she felt a sense of excitement and trepidation. She knew that this journey would not be easy, that there would be challenges and obstacles along the way, but she also knew that it was the right path for her.

As she closed her eyes and took a deep breath, she felt a sense of peace wash over her. She knew that whatever lay ahead, she was ready to face it with an open heart and a clear mind. The journey towards "Union with the Unborn Lord in the Sixth Tower" had begun, and she was ready to embrace it with all her being.

The Light Bringer

As the supernal journey unfolded, a profound realization began to dawn upon me, gradually unraveling the enigmatic nature of the Sixth Tower. It became evident that this towering edifice was not merely a physical structure, but rather a realm of consciousness, an ethereal plane where the soul could transcend the confinements of the material world and attain a profound union with the divine.

With each step I took, a profound transformation unfolded within me. I could feel myself merging with the very essence of existence, a harmonious fusion that transcended the boundaries of time and space. Yet, amidst this ethereal connection, I remained fully present and acutely aware of my surroundings.

However, it was the final surge of ecstasy that proved to be the pinnacle of this extraordinary odyssey. It was as if a blazing inferno of love and luminosity engulfed my entire being, consuming me in its fervent embrace. In that moment, I felt an inexplicable force lifting me beyond the confines of my physical form, beyond the limitations of my mind, and propelling me towards the very core of the Unborn Lord. For an ephemeral instant, I became one with the absolute, an experience so exquisitely profound that it surpassed any other I had ever known.

As the intensity of this celestial wave gradually subsided, I found myself once again inhabiting my physical body. Yet, I knew with unwavering certainty that I had been irrevocably transformed by the ineffable ecstasies of the Sixth Tower. The union with the divine had left an indelible mark upon my soul, forever altering the fabric of my being. A profound sense of peace, love, and joy permeated every fiber of my being, an eternal gift that would accompany me throughout the entirety of my existence.

Then, suddenly, it all came to a crashing halt!

Somehow, through some ignominious means, Aleister Crowley had breached the Sixth Tower gaining access to its inner sanctum. His colossal image materialized before my eyes, engulfing my mind in a whirlwind of confusion and horror. It was a sight that defied comprehension, a grotesque manifestation of power and wickedness that threatened to consume my very soul.

In that moment, I felt a profound sense of helplessness, as if I had been thrust into a nightmarish realm where reality and nightmares intertwined. The enormity of the situation overwhelmed me, leaving me gasping for breath and struggling to make sense of the unfathomable.

The image of Aleister Crowley, with his piercing gaze and twisted smile, seemed to mock my feeble attempts to comprehend the depths of his depravity. It was as if he reveled in the chaos he had unleashed, relishing in the terror that gripped my being.

Abject confusion washed over me, clouding my thoughts and rendering me incapable of rationality. The world around me seemed to blur, as if the very fabric of existence had been torn asunder. I was trapped in a nightmarish limbo, caught between the realms of reality and the macabre fantasies that Crowley embodied.

In that moment, I realized the true extent of his power. He was not merely a man, but a force of darkness that defied all reason and comprehension. And as I stood there, trembling in the face of his malevolence, I knew that the battle ahead would be one of epic proportions, a struggle between light and darkness, good and evil.

But even as I tried to gather my wits and prepare for the worst, I couldn't shake the feeling that it was already too late. Crowley had breached the Sixth Tower, and there was no telling what kind of havoc he would wreak.

I knew that I had to act fast. I had to find a way to stop Crowley before it was too late. But how? The answer eluded me, and I felt a sense of despair creeping in.

In that fateful moment, as the air crackled with anticipation, a celestial force seemed to descend upon me. It was as if a bolt of lightning, forged in the heavens themselves, had struck the very core of my existence.

And there, amidst the ethereal glow, emerged a figure whose presence resonated with an undeniable power. Intuitively, I recognized this enigmatic being as the one destined to vanquish the malevolent sorcery of Crowley. As I stood there, transfixed by the scene unfolding before me, I couldn't help but feel a sense of awe and wonder. The figure before me was like nothing I had ever seen before - his aura was so powerful that it seemed to radiate outwards, enveloping everything in its path.

With unwavering determination, he raised a form of dagger aloft, its gleaming blade reflecting the intensity of his purpose. And then, with a voice that seemed to carry the weight of ancient wisdom, he chanted a mystical mantra that reverberated through the very fabric of reality:

"OM BHASER KILI KILAYA SARVAR BING NE BAM HUM PHET!"

Though the meaning of these sacred words eluded me, their effect was undeniable. In an instant, a radiant barrier materialized, encasing Crowley's wicked form within a mystical triangle. It was a prison of sorts, a metaphysical stronghold that denied him any chance of escape. As if guided by unseen forces, the barrier began to spin, its motion imbued with an otherworldly energy.

With each revolution, the malevolence that had consumed Crowley was stripped away, piece by piece. The darkness that had once shrouded him was banished, replaced by an all-consuming void. And as the barrier completed its final rotation, Crowley was cast into a bottomless abyss, a desolate pit of nothingness.

In that moment, the air grew still, as if the very universe held its breath. The battle against Crowley's evil magick had reached its climax, and victory had been achieved. The presence that had emerged, like a beacon of hope in the darkest of nights, had fulfilled its purpose. And as the echoes of the mystical mantra faded into the ether, a sense of profound relief washed over me, for I knew that my spirit was now free from the clutches of Crowley's malevolence.

My savior was tall and lean, with piercing blue eyes that seemed to see right through you. He wore a simple robe, and his hair was tied back in a loose ponytail. He looked at me with a kind smile, and spoke in a gentle voice.

"My name is Evan, and I'm here to help you complete your spiritual sojourn."

I was grateful to the man who had just saved me from what I thought was certain death. I thanked him profusely, but his response left me puzzled.

He said, "If your true self is Un-born, it will not experience death. Thus, there is no true birth, there is no true death. Only imagined and experienced as very real through the awesome force of the Unborn Mind that is caught within its own creation by its own sustaining and powerful habit-energy."

I was confused and asked him to explain further. "What is this Unborn Mind? Has it something to do with my Union with the Unborn Lord?" I asked.

He replied, "Like the moon above your head. Such is the Unborn Buddha Mind or your true nature. You are now at a junction in your journey that you are ready to enter into Union with IT."

I was intrigued by his words and asked him to elaborate. He explained that the Unborn Mind is the essence of our true nature, which is beyond birth and death. It is the source of all existence and the ultimate reality.

He said that we are all caught up in our own creation, which is sustained by our powerful habit-energy. But if we can tap into the Unborn Mind, we can break free from this cycle of birth and death and attain enlightenment.

I was fascinated by his words and asked him how I could enter into Union with the Unborn Mind. He said that it requires a deep understanding of our true nature and a willingness to let go of our attachments and desires. He said that it is a journey that requires patience, perseverance, and a deep commitment to self-discovery.

I was hesitant as I asked, "Are you absolutely certain that I am prepared for this realization?" The man before me, a wise and experienced teacher, looked at me with a knowing smile and began to explain.

He spoke of a light-trainee, one who walks the earth with a relaxed yet focused demeanor, much like an eagle soaring through the sky with its keen and observant eye. This light-trainee does not allow her mind to depend on anything that is subject to birth and death, and very few situations can affect them. Their sharp dharma-eye can detect even the tiniest of demons crossing their path, revealing their foul nature through their petty actions.

With a calm, detached, and unshakable mind, the light-trainee continues her life calmly and joyfully in whatever she does. The gods themselves bow down to this individual for their wisdom, knowing how foolish they once were when they became gods of pure desire through creating an abundance of good merit.

This light-trainee does not cling to good or bad deeds, and her outflows are tightly shut. There is no hate, passion, or fear within them, yet they are most compassionate in their silence. They are full of life and light, and everyone understands their silent words and enjoys and reveres their presence.

To this light-trainee, the world slowly becomes a world of true spiritual reality, where their true nature abides unmovable and unshakable. Yet, they are lightning-fast when needed, for where their true spirit walks is indeed a most blissful and liberated single point, where neither demons nor gods dare enter.

As I listened to his words, I felt a sense of awe and wonder wash over me. Could I truly become this light-trainee, this blazing light-bringer? The journey ahead seemed daunting, but I knew that with the guidance of this wise teacher, I could begin to walk the path towards true spiritual reality.

The Seventh Tower and Beyond

Pamela, with a sense of accomplishment, believed that her mystical journey had finally reached its conclusion. She had successfully unraveled the enigmatic secrets of the Sixth Tower, which seemed to be the final gateway to enter. However, Evan, a wise companion, gently reassured her that there was still more to be discovered. He explained that the Sixth Tower was not the ultimate destination, for there existed a Seventh Tower that held the key to the ultimate Unborn Unification of mind and spirit.

Pamela's heart fluttered with a mixture of excitement and trepidation at the prospect of continuing her quest. She had already encountered countless trials and tribulations, delving deep into the realms of the mystical and unknown. The journey had tested her resolve, pushing her to the limits of her physical and mental capabilities. Yet, she had persevered, driven by an insatiable curiosity and an unyielding desire to uncover the profound truths that lay hidden within these ancient towers.

Evan, however, knew that her journey was far from over. With a serene smile, he shared his knowledge of the Seventh Tower, a place where the boundaries between the physical and spiritual realms blurred into insignificance. It was said to be a realm of pure-gnosis, where the mind and spirit merged in perfect harmony, transcending the limitations of the mortal world.

Pamela's eyes widened with wonder as she absorbed Evan's words. The prospect of reaching the Seventh Tower ignited a fire within her, fueling her determination to continue the arduous path she had chosen. She knew that this apparent final stage of her mystical odyssey would demand even greater strength, resilience, and unwavering focus.

With renewed purpose, Pamela and Evan set forth on their next adventure undeterred, for they understood that the path to the Seventh Tower was not merely a physical one but a profound inner transformation.

As they drew closer to their destination, they couldn't help but feel a sense of awe and wonder building within them. The towering structure before them seemed to grow larger and more magnificent with each step they took, its grandeur becoming more and more apparent as they approached.

As they gazed up at the towering edifice, they were struck by its sheer size and scale. The tower seemed to stretch up into the heavens, its spire piercing the sky like a needle. The intricate details of its architecture were breathtaking, each curve and angle crafted with the utmost care and precision.

As they drew nearer still, the true majesty of the tower began to reveal itself. The sunlight danced across its surface, casting a warm glow that illuminated every nook and cranny. Pamela couldn't help but feel a sense of reverence and respect for the towering structure before them, as if it were a monument to some long-forgotten deity.

As she and Evan finally reached the base of the tower, they stood in awe of its magnificence. The sheer scale of the structure was overwhelming, and they couldn't help but feel small and insignificant in its shadow. But despite its grandeur, the tower seemed to beckon them forward, inviting them to explore its mysteries and secrets.

And so, with a sense of trepidation and excitement, they began their ascent up the tower, eager to uncover the secrets that lay hidden within its walls.

When Pamela wandered deeper into the Seventh Tower, her eyes fell upon a magnificent scroll, adorned with intricate patterns and shimmering gold accents. It seemed to emanate an otherworldly aura, beckoning her closer.

As the ancient parchment unfurled, it seemed to come alive, as if breathing with a life of its own. The room was filled with an ethereal glow, casting dancing shadows on the walls.

And there, in elegant calligraphy, the scroll unveiled its awe-inspiring message.

In the majestic Seventh Tower, the soul finds itself in a state of profound revelation, as if standing face to face with the very essence of existence itself. Here, the Absolute Stature of the Unborn takes form, revealing its divine presence through the manifestation of the Blessed Three Jewels: Dharmakaya Buddha, the embodiment of ultimate truth and wisdom; the splendid Word of the Buddhadharma, a sacred teaching that illuminates the path to enlightenment; and the Mystical Community of the Illuminative Light of the Unborn, a gathering of enlightened beings radiating the brilliance of the Unborn's wisdom.

Within the confines of this ethereal tower, the soul's perception expands beyond the limitations of the physical realm, allowing it to witness the boundless nature of the Unborn. It is a sight that transcends ordinary vision, for it is an encounter with the very essence of existence itself.

Dharmakaya Buddha, the first of the Blessed Three Jewels, stands as a symbol of the Unborn's eternal wisdom and truth. In his presence, the soul is enveloped by a profound sense of clarity and understanding, as if all the mysteries of the universe are unveiled before its very eyes. The wisdom emanating from Dharmakaya Buddha is not mere knowledge, but a transformative force that awakens the dormant potential within the soul, guiding it towards the path of enlightenment.

The splendid Word of the Buddhadharma, the second Jewel, resonates within the Seventh Tower, filling the air with its sacred vibrations. This divine teaching, passed down through generations, carries the essence of the Unborn's wisdom, offering guidance and illumination to those who seek the truth. As the soul listens to the resonating words, it feels a deep resonance within its being, as if every cell is attuned to the cosmic harmony of the Unborn's eternal message.

Finally, the Mystical Community of the Illuminative Light of the Unborn, the third Jewel, gathers within the Seventh Tower. This community is comprised of enlightened beings who have transcended the limitations of the physical realm, radiating the brilliance of the Unborn's wisdom. Their presence is awe-inspiring, as their illuminated forms emit a divine light that permeates every corner of the tower. In their company, the soul feels a sense of belonging and unity, as if it has found its true home amidst the vastness of the Unborn's creation.

In this realm of supernality, there exists a remarkable illustration of the Unmoving Principle. It is none other than IT, a celestial entity that remains steadfast and resolute, refusing to yield to the forces of motion. This ethereal beingness resides in the heaven of all heavens, a sacred abode where no disruptive movement dares to intrude.

Within this celestial sanctuary, a profound stillness permeates the atmosphere, creating an ambiance of tranquility and serenity. It is a place where the very essence of motion is held at bay, unable to disturb the delicate balance that reigns supreme. Here, the laws of physics seem to bow down in reverence, acknowledging the sovereignty of the Unmoving Principle.

In this heavenly realm, the concept of hindrance is but a distant memory. No external force can dare to challenge the unwavering nature of IT. It stands as a testament to the power of immobility, a symbol of unwavering strength and stability. The celestial beings that inhabit this realm marvel at IT, for it embodies the epitome of steadfastness.

As one gazes upon IT, a sense of awe and wonder fills the heart. How can something so resolute and unyielding exist in a world dominated by constant change and flux? It is a question that elicits contemplation and introspection, for IT defies the very nature of existence itself.

In the grand tapestry of the cosmos, IT stands as a beacon of stillness, a guiding light amidst the chaos of movement. It serves as a reminder that amidst the ebb and flow of life, there exists a realm untouched by the tumultuous currents of change. IT is a sanctuary for those seeking solace from the relentless march of time.

In this celestial haven, the Unmoving Principle reigns supreme, unchallenged by the forces of motion. It is a testament to the eternal nature of existence, a glimpse into a realm where disturbances are but a distant memory. As we contemplate the significance of IT, we are reminded of the beauty and power that lies in stillness, and the profound impact it can have on our lives.

Pamela had finally achieved her Divine Union with the Unborn, a momentous occasion that Evan felt deserved a fitting tribute. With a sense of reverence, he spoke the words that would forever mark this moment in time. "One dwells now in the center—the sanctum sanctorum of the Unborn Mind," he declared. It was a powerful statement that spoke to the depth of Pamela's spiritual journey and the significance of this milestone.

Evan went on to explain that this Holy Communion was complete and forever sealed against all evil. It was a moment of pure transcendence, a state of being that was beyond the reach of any negative force. The former ravaging discursive mindset that had plagued Pamela for so long was finally silenced. In its place was a sense of perpetual Spiritual Tranquility, a state of being that would remain with her always.

As Evan spoke, the room was filled with a sense of awe and wonder. It was clear that something truly remarkable had taken place, something that would forever change the course of Pamela's life. And as she basked in the glow of this moment, she knew that she had truly found her place in the world, a place of peace and harmony that would sustain her for all time.

Pamela's eyes sparkled with excitement as she exclaimed, her voice filled with pure delight, "Oh, how absolutely succulent the Absolute Center of the Unborn Mind is!" Her words resonated with a profound sense of awe and wonder, as if she had just stumbled upon a hidden treasure of immeasurable value. The sheer joy that radiated from her was infectious, captivating the audience of the Seventh Tower all around her. It was as if she had unlocked a secret door to a realm of unimaginable bliss, and she couldn't contain her enthusiasm. The Absolute Center of the Unborn Mind, a Self-realization so profound and elusive, had finally revealed itself to her, and she couldn't help but revel in its magnificence.

After a long and arduous journey, she finally reached her destination. The exhaustion that had settled deep within her bones was momentarily forgotten as she let out a triumphant exclamation, "I've made it at last!" The weight of her accomplishment lifted from her shoulders, replaced by a sense of pride and fulfillment.

However, her moment of celebration was interrupted by the voice of Evan, a wise and experienced spiritual mentor. With a gentle yet firm tone, he reminded her, "You've met the mark of Union, yes, but your journey as a Light-Bringer, a Bodhisattva, is far from over. In fact, it is just beginning."

His words hung in the air, causing her excitement to waver and a flicker of uncertainty to creep into her heart. She had believed that reaching this milestone would mark the end of her mission, that she had fulfilled her purpose. But Evan's words shattered that illusion, revealing a deeper truth she had yet to comprehend.

As she looked into his eyes, she saw a profound wisdom and compassion that emanated from within him. It was a reminder of the immense responsibility she now carried as a Light-Bringer, a beacon of hope and enlightenment for others. The weight of this realization settled upon her, replacing her initial elation with a newfound determination.

Evan continued, his voice filled with encouragement, "Your journey has only just begun, my dear. As a Bodhisattva, you are tasked with guiding others towards the path of enlightenment, bringing light to those lost in darkness. Your purpose is to alleviate suffering and spread compassion throughout the world."

Her mind raced, trying to comprehend the magnitude of her role. She had always known that her calling was to make a difference, to bring about positive change. But now, standing at the precipice of her destiny, she understood that her purpose was far greater than she had ever imagined.

With a deep breath, she nodded, accepting the weight of her new mission. The road ahead would be challenging, filled with obstacles and uncertainties. Yet, she was ready to embrace her role as a Light-Bringer, to embark on a journey that would test her strength, resilience, and unwavering commitment to the greater good.

As she looked out into the horizon, a sense of purpose and determination filled her being. The mark of Union was just the beginning, a stepping stone towards a greater destiny. With Evan by her side, she knew she would find the strength to persevere.

Part Three

The Five Rogues

As Evan and Pamela traversed the illustrious path of the Unborn Odyssey, Evan found himself lost in thought, reminiscing about his own journey towards Self-realization within the Unborn scheme of things. He began to share his experiences with Pamela, recounting his initial encounters with the Primordial. Evan spoke of his former Ch'an Master, who had guided him towards a deeper understanding of the Unborn, and the gnome-like entity that resided within his own mysterious Tower of Illumination, who had imparted further teachings upon him.

Evan continued to recount his journey, speaking of the further unknown primordial beings who had shared their wisdom with him, and the challenges he had faced along the way. Despite the difficulties, Evan had persevered, and had ultimately achieved the pinnacle of Buddhagnosis by climbing the Ten-fold Lankavatarian path of Noble Self-realization.

As Evan spoke, Pamela listened intently, fascinated by his journey and the knowledge he had gained. Together, they continued down the path of the Unborn Odyssey, eager to discover what lay ahead.

As the two companions continued on their journey together, they came across a multitude of beings who were trapped in their own ignorance. These creatures were unable to grasp the life-saving illumination of the Unborn, which had the power to release them from the chains they had created for themselves. The duo encountered a diverse range of these captives, each with their own unique characteristics and struggles. Despite their differences, they all shared the same inability to comprehend the freeing light of the Unborn. It was often a frustrating and disheartening experience for the travelers, who longed to help these beings break free from their self-imposed limitations. As they journeyed on, another unknown traveler joined them. This new traveler sported a bulbous mustache and wore clothing that showed signs of a long and tiring journey.

As they continued on their way, the new traveler began to sense their frustration and their struggle to understand the nature of the beast. With a deep understanding of the path of the Unborn, the traveler explained that a puthujjana is a spiritually blind person who cannot distinguish a noble person from a non-noble person.

The reason for this, the traveler explained, is that a puthujjana cannot sense the spiritual presence of a noble person. Even if a Buddha or a recent current-winner were sitting among them in a Dharma center, no one would be able to recognize them because they are puthujjanas who lack the dharma-eye.

The dharma-eye, the traveler continued, marks entry into the supermundane path which is the true Buddhist way. Here's the full teaching in parable form:

"Once upon a time, in a realm where ancient wisdom and spiritual practices thrived, there existed a profound belief in the power of removal. This practice, known as the via negativa, held the key to unlocking one's true identity and ultimately achieving a state of profound resonance, known as samadhi.

"The via negativa taught that our journey towards self-discovery required us to detach ourselves from the world around us. It emphasized that our physical bodies, intricately intertwined with the external realm, encompassed what was known as the Five Aggregates. These aggregates, comprising form, sensation, perception, mental formations, and consciousness, were the very essence of our existence. And yet, paradoxically, they were also the very obstacles that needed to be eliminated.

"As sentient beings, we found ourselves deeply entangled in the intricate web of this grand illusion. Our attachment to the physical world and our own bodies was so profound that we lacked the ability to extricate ourselves from it through sheer willpower alone. The mere thought of someone threatening our physical form would send waves of overwhelming terror coursing through our veins.

"It was within this context that the practice of removal gained its significance. By gradually shedding the layers of attachment and illusion, one could inch closer to their true essence. The remover, as they embarked on this arduous journey, would peel away the external distractions and delve deeper into the core of their being. With each step taken on this path, they would inch closer to their authentic self, resonating with it in a profound and transformative way.

"The ultimate goal was to achieve samadhi, a state of complete absorption and unity with one's true identity. In this state, the remover would transcend the limitations of the physical world and experience a profound sense of oneness with the universe. The removal of the external and the dissolution of the false self would pave the way for a spiritual awakening of unparalleled magnitude.

"Yet, the path towards removal was not for the faint of heart. It demanded unwavering dedication, discipline, and a willingness to confront the deepest fears and attachments that held us captive. It required us to confront the very essence of our existence and question the illusions that had shaped our perception of reality.

"For within the realm of removal, the remover embarked on a journey of self-discovery that went beyond the confines of the physical body. It was a quest to uncover the true nature of our being, to transcend the limitations of attachment and ignorance, and to find solace in the boundless expanse of the spiritual realm."

And so with this newfound understanding, Evan and Pamela bowed and thanked the traveler and continued on their journey with a renewed sense of purpose and a deeper understanding of the path they were on.

As they delved deeper into their spiritual journey, a profound realization began to take root within their hearts. It became clear to them that the true villain responsible for the perpetual state of ignorance was none other than the Five Skandhas, those insidious aspects of human existence that held an ignominious grip on all sentient reality.

With this newfound understanding, they recognized that the key to achieving authentic Noble Self-realization lay in dismantling the stronghold of these Skandhas. Their disbanding was not merely a matter of choice, but a crucial step towards liberation from the shackles of suffering.

Each of the Five Skandhas represented a different facet of human experience, and together they formed the very foundation of one's identity. The first Skandha, form, encompassed the physical body and its sensory perceptions. The second, sensation, encompassed the myriad feelings and emotions that arose from these perceptions. The third, perception, involved the categorization and interpretation of these sensations. The fourth, mental formations, encompassed the thoughts, beliefs, and volitions that shaped one's actions. And finally, consciousness, the fifth Skandha, represented the awareness that tied all these aspects together.

It was through the interplay of these Skandhas that the illusion of a separate self was perpetuated, leading to attachment, aversion, and ultimately, suffering. They realized that by disbanding these Skandhas, they could dismantle the very foundation of their ego-driven existence, paving the way for true awakening.

However, this was no easy task. The Skandhas had woven themselves intricately into the fabric of their being, entangled in every thought, every emotion, and every perception. To disband them required a deep and unwavering commitment to self-inquiry, mindfulness, and the cultivation of wisdom.

With each passing day, they embarked on an enhanced journey of self-discovery, peeling away the layers of conditioning and illusion that had kept them bound for so long. They observed the arising and passing away of sensations, emotions, and thoughts, recognizing their impermanence and inherent emptiness. Gradually, they began to loosen the grip of the Skandhas, untangling the web of identification that had ensnared them.

As the Skandhas dissolved, sentient beings would experience a profound shift in their perception of reality. No longer confined by the limitations of these five rogues, they began to see the interconnectedness of all things, the interdependence of every being set free in the very heart of Noble Wisdom.

The Abyss

Pamela and Evan found themselves standing before a deep pit, blocking their path. As they peered down into the depths of the pit, their eyes widened in shock and horror. A vast sea of writhing, squirming bodies filled the space below, each one desperately clawing and scrabbling at the walls in a frenzied attempt to escape.

At first, they couldn't quite make out what they were seeing. The creatures below were unlike anything they had ever encountered before - strange, twisted forms that seemed to blur the line between animal and human. Some had multiple limbs, others had tentacles or wings or tails. Some were covered in fur or scales or feathers, while others were slick and slimy to the touch.

But despite their differences, all of the creatures shared one thing in common: a fierce determination to climb their way out of the pit and back into the world above.

As they watched, transfixed, the creatures began to surge forward in a massive wave, their bodies pressing against each other in a desperate bid for freedom. The noise was deafening - a cacophony of grunts and groans and snarls and screams that echoed off the walls of the pit and reverberated through the air.

As they peered into its depths and the disordered confusion, they soon discerned that it was all a metaphor for something much deeper and profound. They believed that this pit represented the realization that ignorance, known as avidya in influential circles, had roots that ran far beneath the surface. It was as if there existed an unconscious repository within it, filled with tainted seeds.

This repository, they discerned, was called the Alaya-vijnana or "storehouse consciousness." It held within it all the karmic sensate data that had accumulated since time immemorial. Like the calm surface of the ocean, the Alaya-vijnana remained undisturbed in itself. However, when influenced by the waves of the Vijnanas, the elements of consciousness, it set samsara, the cycle of birth and death, into motion.

As they gazed into its abyss, they couldn't help but feel a sense of awe and trepidation. In that moment, Pamela and Evan realized that this pit was not just a physical entity, but a metaphor for their own personal journey. It represented the never-ending quest for self-discovery, a journey that would take them deep into the recesses of their own consciousness. They understood that this was not a path for the faint-hearted, but one that required courage, determination, and an unwavering commitment to uncovering the truth.

They knew that this journey would not be easy. It would demand that they confront their deepest fears, their darkest secrets, and their most hidden desires. It would force them to question their beliefs, challenge their assumptions, and confront the limitations of their own ignorance. But they were willing to embark on this path, for they understood that only by delving into the depths of their own being could they hope to attain the enlightened state of Buddhahood.

Before they ventured onward, though, Evan and Pamela could not but feel deep sympathy and compassion for the squirming inhabitants of the abyss. As "Light Bringers", Bodhisattvas, Evan and Pamela were no strangers to the suffering of others. They knew that it was their duty to help alleviate the pain and misery of those around them, no matter how great the challenge.

And so, before they ventured onward, Evan and Pamela decided to take a moment to help the inhabitants of the abyss. They closed their eyes and focused their minds, calling upon the power of the Unborn Light to heal and soothe the suffering creatures below.

With a great burst of energy, they generated waves of healing light that flowed down into the abyss, bathing the creatures in a warm and comforting glow. For a brief moment, the squirming inhabitants were able to find some relief from their pain and suffering.

As the sun began to set on the horizon, casting a warm golden glow over the weary travelers, they turned to face the path that lay ahead. The air was filled with a sense of accomplishment, a deep-rooted satisfaction that emanated from within their souls. They had done what they could, gone above and beyond to lend a helping hand to those in need.

Their ongoing journey continued to be long and arduous, fraught with challenges and obstacles that seemed insurmountable at times. Yet, each time they had persevered, driven by an unwavering determination to make a difference in the lives of others. Their hearts had been touched by the stories of struggle and hardship they had encountered along the way, and they had vowed to do whatever it took to alleviate the suffering they witnessed.

With each passing day, their resolve had grown stronger, their compassion deeper. They had shared their meager provisions with the hungry, offered shelter to the homeless, and provided solace to the broken-hearted. They had listened to the tales of despair and offered words of encouragement, reminding those they encountered that they were not alone in their struggles.

Now, as they stood at this crossroad, their bodies weary and their spirits uplifted, they couldn't help but feel a profound sense of fulfillment. They had given their all, poured their hearts and souls into this noble mission, and the impact they had made was immeasurable. The smiles they had witnessed, the tears they had wiped away, and the gratitude they had received were etched into their memories, forever reminding them of the power of compassion and selflessness.
As they gazed into the distance, the road stretched out before them, winding its way through lush green fields and towering mountains. It was a path that held countless unknowns, challenges yet to be faced, and lives yet to be touched. But they were not afraid. They had learned that the true reward lay not in the destination, but in the journey itself.

With renewed determination, they took their first steps forward, their hearts filled with hope and their souls brimming with a sense of purpose. They knew that there were still countless souls out there, waiting for a helping hand, a kind word, or a simple act of kindness. And they were ready to continue their mission, to spread love and compassion wherever they went.

As they embarked on this new leg of their journey, they carried with them the memories of those they had helped, the lives they had touched. And they knew that no matter how challenging the road ahead may be, they were made to make a difference.

The Pregnancy

One fateful day, Pamela approached Evan with a revelation that would forever alter the course of their lives. She declared that she was pregnant, a statement that left Evan dumbfounded. How could this be? They had never engaged in any intimate relations. Confusion and disbelief clouded Evan's mind as he tried to comprehend the situation. Yet, Pamela remained resolute, insisting that she was indeed carrying some form of pregnancy, though uncertain of its nature.

As Evan grappled with the perplexing circumstances, a sudden realization dawned upon him. He had experienced something similar in his own spiritual journey. The concept of a "spiritual pregnancy" suddenly made sense to him. It was a profound revelation, a realization that went beyond the physical realm.

With newfound clarity, Evan turned to Pamela and began to share his understanding. He spoke of a treasure, a radiant pearl that existed alongside this spiritual pregnancy. It awaited its immaculate birth, a birth that transcended the limitations of mortal existence in a harsh and unforgiving world.

Evan explained that many mistakenly believed that everyone possessed the Buddha-nature or that they themselves were Buddhas. However, this was not the case. He recounted how Buddha Gotama had pointed directly at individuals, emphasizing that they all held the potential to discover the seed of the Buddha within themselves. By focusing their attention, cultivating right view, right concentration, and right effort, they could nourish the growth of this spiritual seed.

Drawing upon the experiences of mothers and women, Evan conveyed the immense care and attention required during the process of bringing forth a child. Similarly, those who chose to participate in this spiritual birth would be astounded by the radiant light that emanated when their true selves were born as bodhisattvas. It was a moment beyond comparison, transcending the boundaries of the earthly realm.

Evan went on to explain that this newborn spiritual child would undergo ten stages before attaining Buddhahood. However, there was no need for concern, as the process unfolded naturally. The key was to allow the light to flow steadily from this child as it grew. Eventually, the awakened spiritual child would sever the cord connecting it to its false "twin," the Alaya vijnana, thus embarking on the great path destined for all bodhisattvas before fully recollecting their Buddhahood.

The decision to become a birth-giver is not one to be taken lightly. It requires a deep understanding of the spiritual responsibility that comes with such a role. Only the Unborn, the creator of all things, is able to conceive such a birth. If you choose to become a birth-giver, you must prepare a spiritual "womb" in which the seed can mature and eventually reach its predestined future as a Buddha.

It is important to understand that a potential Buddha does not already reside within you. A Buddha cannot exist within a composition of karmic defilements such as desires, emotions, and memories. To believe otherwise is to invite spiritual trouble.

The Buddha Nature is already present in Dharmadhatu, the True Nature of Reality, waiting for the spiritual child to be born and fully recollect it. It is not a personal path, and the false notion that there is a specific path for each being should be left behind. There is only one path to liberation, and the Buddha Gotama showed us how to awaken our true selves and enter the 10-stage bodhisattvic path, allowing ourselves to evolve into a Tathagata.

Becoming a birth-giver is a profound spiritual journey that requires dedication, preparation, and a deep understanding of the nature of existence. It is not a decision to be taken lightly, but for those who are willing to undertake the journey, the rewards are immeasurable.

Pamela's heart swelled with an overwhelming sense of joy and anticipation as she received the news that she was carrying within her the precious gift of a "Spiritual Child" of Light, a Bodhichild. This revelation filled her with a profound sense of purpose and responsibility, knowing that she had been chosen to nurture and guide this divine being.

Evan, her wise and trusted mentor, had shared with her the significance of this extraordinary occurrence. He explained that the birth of a Bodhichild was a rare and sacred event, a manifestation of enlightenment itself. Pamela was humbled by the magnitude of this revelation, realizing that she had been entrusted with a profound spiritual task.

Evan, with his gentle and reassuring voice, emphasized the importance of preparing her own Dharma-womb, or Tathagata-garbha, as he called it. He explained that this metaphorical womb represented the fertile ground within her being, where the seeds of enlightenment could take root and flourish. Pamela listened intently, absorbing every word, determined to create the perfect environment for her Bodhichild to grow and thrive.

With Evan's guidance, Pamela embarked on a journey of self-discovery and transformation. She delved deep into the teachings of the Buddha, immersing herself in the wisdom of the ages. She meditated for hours on end, seeking inner stillness and clarity. She embraced the practice of mindfulness, cultivating a heightened awareness of the present moment.

Days turned into weeks, and weeks into months, as Pamela diligently prepared her Dharma-womb. She purified her thoughts, letting go of negativity and embracing compassion and love. She cultivated a serene and harmonious environment, surrounding herself with beauty and tranquility.

Throughout this arduous yet rewarding process, Evan stood by Pamela's side, offering guidance and encouragement. He reminded her that the birth of the Bodhichild was not the end, but rather the beginning of a new chapter in her spiritual journey. Once the child of light emerged into the world, it would become her steadfast companion, guiding her towards the ultimate goal of full Buddhahood.

Pamela's heart swelled with gratitude for the opportunity bestowed upon her. She felt a deep connection to the Bodhichild growing within her, sensing its presence as a beacon of hope and enlightenment. With each passing day, her anticipation grew, knowing that soon she would witness the miraculous birth of this divine being, not through a normal womb birth, but through a spiritual-womb, even more profound.

Birthing the Bodhichild

Pamela had a conversation with Evan where she expressed that she was feeling an intense inner light that was causing her to feel like she was about to burst. Evan explained to her that this was a sign that the Bodhichild, the child of Unborn Light, was about to be born. In order to properly prepare for this birth, Pamela needed to learn how to regulate her breathing through a practice known as Spirit Breathing.

Evan explained that when the Bodhichild stirs, it triggers the development of proper breathing. This involves uniting the Qi, or life force energy, with the mind. To achieve this, one must make use of two essential lights: the Light of Yang and the Translucent Light of Yin. The Light of Yang represents the exuberance of the Qi energies, like the golden furnace of the sun, while the Translucent Light of Yin represents the inner luminosity, like the luminous surface of the moon. Both of these lights share the same spiritual core of the One Mind and Absolute.

To begin Spirit Breathing, one must meditate and focus on the dantian point, which is located two finger points below the navel. By doing this, one relinquishes control of the Body-Consciousness and begins to listen to the heart beat of the Child of Light. This is the start of the inner-listening that is necessary for Spirit Breathing.

In the ancient teachings, there is a beautiful analogy that perfectly captures the interconnectedness of all things. It is said that the mother hen is able to successfully hatch her eggs because she is constantly attuned to the development of her chicks. While it may seem like she is simply providing warmth to the outer shell, her deep focus and attention also generate an inner heat, a flow of vital energy known as Qi, which nurtures and incubates the growing embryos.

Even when the mother hen momentarily leaves the eggs, she does so with an attitude of attentive listening, always ready to return and continue her nurturing role. This unwavering focus is akin to the unbroken concentration of the Primordial Spirit, the essence of our being.

For the adept who is fully aware and awake, this process of "spiritual-hatching" within the mind signifies the death of the carnal mind, the ego-driven self. But it also heralds a supreme awakening, a profound realization of the Undivided Mind, the state of unity and oneness with all existence.

As one transitions from mundane breathing to the inner-circulation of Qi energies emanating from the heart of the Bodhichild, the sound of respiration fades away. Instead, one listens for the silent flow of a softer breath that is a much subtler and supple-Mind. This is known as "True-Breathing" and it penetrates to the ultimate truths of Spiritual-Awareness. The Bodhichild now does the breathing through the practitioner, and the Bodhi-mind and breath become inextricably linked. This creates a sense of quietude in the mind and spirit.

The final step is to "turn the Light around" and allow the Bodhichild to be born. This involves a reversal of the Light away from defiled-dharma and a self-emptying of all that is malignant. By doing this, the Bodhichild can be born and the practitioner can achieve a higher level of spiritual awareness.

When the Bodhichild blossoms in Its Womb of Deathless-Suchness, transcendence from the samsaric-spin of life and death is assured. This means that one can exchange mundane-breathing for the inner-circulation of the Qi-energies which are now emanating from the heart of the Bodhichild. This transition is so subtle that if it occurs unheeded, one no longer hears the sound of respiration. Instead, one simply turns-about the breathing and hearing and listens for the silent-flow of a softer breath of that much subtler and supple-Mind. This empowers "True-Breathing", one that penetrates to the ultimate truths of Spiritual-Awareness. This translates as the Bodhichild now doing the breathing through you....hence, the Bodhichild is born.

Pamela commenced the practice of Spirit Breathing for an extended duration. She had been working hard to achieve the state where the Bodhichild blossoms in Its Womb of Deathless-Suchness. And finally, after much effort, she felt a sudden explosion of Joy! "I can feel it," she exclaimed, "It is being birthed!" She could sense the subtle energies emanating from the heart of the Bodhichild, and she knew that she had achieved a state of transcendence from the samsaric-spin of life and death. She was now empowered with "True-Breathing", one that penetrated to the ultimate truths of Spiritual-Awareness. The Bodhichild was now doing the breathing through her, and she felt a deep sense of peace and contentment.

Pamela's eyes sparkled with excitement as she turned to face Evan, her voice filled with awe and wonder. "Oh, Evan," she exclaimed, her words bursting forth with an infectious enthusiasm, "I cannot even begin to express the overwhelming joy that fills my heart at the mere thought of experiencing the birth of this Child of Unborn Light!"

Her words hung in the air, carrying a sense of profound anticipation. Pamela's deep reverence for this momentous event was evident in every fiber of her being. The Unborn Light of Light, a concept so ethereal and mystical, held a special place in her heart. It was a beacon of hope, a symbol of purity and enlightenment that transcended the boundaries of human comprehension.

As she spoke, her voice quivered with a mixture of excitement and reverence. The Bodhichild represented the very essence of divinity, an embodiment of all that was good and pure in the world. To witness its birth was a privilege beyond measure, a rare opportunity to glimpse the infinite beauty that lay beyond the realm of mortal existence.

Pamela's eyes shone with a radiant glow as she continued, her words flowing like a gentle stream of consciousness. "Imagine, Evan, the sheer brilliance that will illuminate the world as the Unborn Light of Light emerges from the depths of the unknown. It will be a moment of pure transcendence, a revelation that will forever alter the course of our lives."

Her voice grew softer, almost reverential, as she spoke of the profound impact this event would have on their souls. "To witness the birth of the Child of Unborn Light is to be touched by the divine, to experience a connection to something greater than ourselves. It is a reminder that there is a purpose to our existence, a higher calling that beckons us to seek truth and enlightenment."

Pamela's words hung in the air, enveloping them both in a cocoon of anticipation. The Unborn Light of Light, a concept so abstract and intangible, had become a tangible reality in her mind. It was a beacon of hope, a guiding light that would lead her towards a deeper understanding of the cosmos and her place within it.

As they stood there, on the precipice of this extraordinary event, Pamela and Evan shared a silent understanding. They knew that witnessing the birth of the Unborn Light of Light would be a transformative experience, one that would forever change the way she perceived the world.

With hearts filled to the brim with anticipation, they embarked on a remarkable odyssey, venturing deeper into the enigmatic realm known as the Undiscovered Country of the Unborn. The air crackled with an electric energy as they pressed forward, their souls ablaze with curiosity and wonder.

As they journeyed further, the landscape transformed before their very eyes. The once familiar surroundings gave way to an ethereal realm, where time seemed to stand still. The air was thick with an otherworldly mist, casting an eerie glow upon their path. Every step they took felt like a leap into the unknown, as if they were treading upon the threshold of a secret world.

Their senses heightened, attuned to the subtle whispers of the Unborn. They could almost hear the faint echoes of unborn dreams and aspirations, mingling with the gentle rustling of leaves. It was as if the very essence of life itself was pulsating through the air, urging them to delve deeper into the mysteries that lay ahead.

With each passing moment, their anticipation grew, fueled by the tantalizing prospect of uncovering the secrets that had eluded humanity for centuries. They were driven by an insatiable thirst for knowledge, a burning desire to unravel the enigma of the Unborn.

The path they followed was treacherous, winding through dense forests and crossing treacherous rivers. Yet, their determination remained unyielding, their spirits unbroken. They were explorers of the mind, pioneers of the soul, and nothing could deter them from their quest.

As they ventured deeper into the heart of the Undiscovered Country, they encountered breathtaking sights that defied imagination. Majestic mountains soared towards the heavens, their peaks shrouded in a mystical haze. Crystal-clear lakes mirrored the sky above, reflecting the infinite possibilities that lay within the Unborn.

With each passing day, they felt a profound connection to the Unborn, as if they were peering into the very essence of existence itself. They marveled at the boundless potential that resided within this ethereal realm, where dreams were yet to be dreamt and destinies were yet to be forged.

Their odyssey was not without its challenges, for the Unborn guarded its secrets fiercely. They faced trials that tested their resolve, pushing them to their limits. Yet, they persevered, fueled by an unwavering belief that the answers they sought were within their grasp.

Archway of the Black Dragons

As the sun began to set, casting a warm golden glow over a tranquil garden, Evan found himself engrossed in a deep conversation with Pamela. They sat on a weathered wooden bench, surrounded by vibrant flowers and the gentle rustling of leaves. Evan, with a thoughtful expression on his face, began to articulate to Pamela the profound nature of The Black Dragons.

With each word that escaped his lips, Evan's voice carried a sense of reverence and awe. He spoke of the ancient wisdom that had been passed down through generations, the teachings that had shaped the very essence of The Black Dragons. As he delved deeper into his narrative, his eyes sparkled with a mixture of excitement and respect.

"The Buddha nature," Evan began, his voice filled with a sense of wonder, "is at the core of The Black Dragons. It is the guiding force that leads us on our path of self-discovery and enlightenment, accompanied with an inconceivable wisdom." He paused for a moment, allowing his words to sink in before continuing.

He described how The Black Dragons, some also revered in the martial arts, had embraced the teachings of the Buddha to cultivate not only physical strength but also spiritual growth. Their training went beyond mere combat techniques; it encompassed a holistic approach to life, emphasizing the importance of inner peace and harmony.

Evan's words painted a vivid picture of the Black Dragons' training grounds, nestled amidst towering mountains and cascading waterfalls. He spoke of the rigorous discipline and unwavering dedication that each member of the elite group possessed, as they sought to embody the Buddha's teachings in every aspect of their lives.

Pamela listened intently, her eyes fixed on Evan's animated face. She could sense the passion and sincerity in his words, and it ignited a curiosity within her. She yearned to understand more about this ancient philosophy that had shaped the lives of the Black Dragons.

As the evening wore on, Evan continued to weave his narrative, sharing anecdotes of legendary masters who had walked the path before them. He spoke of their unwavering commitment to compassion, wisdom, and selflessness, and how these virtues had become the cornerstone of The Black Dragons' existence.

With each passing moment, Pamela found herself drawn deeper into the world Evan described. The garden around them seemed to fade away, replaced by visions of a grand temple where the Black Dragons gathered to meditate and train. She could almost feel the energy and serenity that permeated the air, as if the very essence of the Buddha's teachings had taken physical form.

Evan spoke with a sense of awe and reverence as he described the incredible wisdom that filled the minds of those who had transcended the sensory addicted mind. He used a metaphor of a birdcage, explaining that when the illusion of the false bird dies and the cage is opened, the virtuous one is able to recollect the unborn essence. This allows them to find the gateless gate to their original source of perfection, transcending all delusions of duality or nonduality.

Evan went on to explain that this ability to transcend the sensory addicted mind is the greatest quality and truth of the Black Dragon. There is no delusion to reject and no things to transcend, all things are equal and thus sunyata, and obstructive notions of closed or open minds are eternally ceased.

The Black Dragon, a magnificent defender of the true law, is able to cut off a thousand heads from heretic misconceptions. This allows the true lotus to blossom on its own accord, with the mind unbound, uncreated, and radiating in all ten directions, perfectly illuminating a thousand dharmas. Evan questioned how petty desire or delusion of the worldling could ever recollect such a thousand fold instant wisdom.

He explained that the most sacred and unborn mani-pearl is always radiant and clear, and it is not for anyone to defile its original bright nature with notions of good or evil. The pure desire to awake is what drove Prince Gautama to recollect what was always there for him, guided by the light of countless Tathagatas.

Evan described how, by allowing the true essence to antecede personal experience, one can enter the luminous non-personal way of the Thus come Thus gone. This is obscured and hidden to the ordinary sensory clinging mind. The form skandha is transcended, all bodies of desire vanish, and the sensation skandha is transcended, revealing the vanity of grasping. The conceptual skandha is bypassed, and notions of life and death are ceased. The volition skandha is calmed, allowing for perfect freedom to free the suffering. The sensory consciousness is crushed, and the foul architect instantly evaporated.

Evan concluded by saying that Black Dragons like Bodhidharma and Tsung-Mi intended to enable people to realize the dark penetration. They point straight at the secret entrance of the dragon's lair, leading to the principle of the Undivided Luminosity of the Unborn Mind and Spirit.

As the sun began its descent, casting a warm golden glow across the land, Evan stood at the edge of a vast field. His outstretched arm pointed towards the horizon, where the setting sun painted a breathtaking scene. A magnificent Archway, stretching high into the heavens, seemed to beckon them forward.

With a glimmer of excitement in his eyes, Evan turned to Pamela and spoke with a voice filled with anticipation. "Once we cross the threshold of that celestial Archway," he declared, his words carrying a sense of wonder, "we shall find ourselves in the esteemed presence of the legendary Black Dragons."

His words hung in the air, mingling with the gentle breeze that rustled the grass beneath their feet. They exchanged glances, their hearts pounding with a mixture of trepidation and curiosity. The allure of the unknown, the promise of adventure, tugged at their souls.

The Black Dragons, whispered about in hushed tones among the adventurous souls, were also said to possess extraordinary powers. Legends spoke of their ability to shape destinies, to wield magic that could alter the course of history. To be in their noble company was a privilege sought by many, yet attained by few.

As Evan and Pamela stood at the precipice of this unknown realm, their hearts filled with a mixture of hope and trepidation. They knew that crossing the barrier of the celestial Archway would not be an ordinary journey. It would require courage, determination, and a willingness to embrace the unknown.

With a final glance at one another, they took a collective breath and stepped forward, their feet carrying them towards the radiant Archway. Each step brought them closer to a destiny intertwined with the fabled Black Dragons. The sun dipped lower, casting long shadows behind them, as they embarked on a journey that would forever enhance their spiritual quest.

Convocation of the Noble Ones

As Pamela and Evan approached the grand entrance of the magnificent golden Archway, they couldn't help but feel a sense of awe and wonder. The archway was adorned with intricate carvings of dragons, their scales shimmering in the sunlight. As they stepped through the archway, they were greeted by a group of regal-looking Black Dragons, each one towering over them.

They were led through a long hallway, the walls adorned with tapestries depicting scenes of great spiritual battles and heroic deeds in countless Buddhafields. The air was thick with the scent of incense, and the sound of chanting filled their ears. Finally, they arrived at the entrance to the Great Spiritual Hall of the Noble Black Dragons.

The hall was unlike anything they had ever seen before. The walls were lined with glowing crystals, casting a soft, ethereal light throughout the room. In the center of the hall stood a massive statue of a black dragon, its eyes seeming to follow their every move. They were then led to a pair of ornate chairs, and they sat down, feeling both honored and humbled to be in the presence of such honored beings.

As the sun began its descent below the horizon, casting a warm golden glow over the land, a hushed anticipation filled the air. The atmosphere crackled with an electric energy, as if the very universe held its breath in anticipation of what was to come. It was a splendid evening, one that would forever be etched in the memories of those fortunate enough to bear witness.

And then, as if summoned by some unseen force, they began to arrive. From every corner of existence, beings of unimaginable wisdom and enlightenment converged upon the sacred grounds. The Great Convocation was about to commence, a gathering of such magnitude that it would forever alter the course of spiritual history.

Bodhisattvas, with their serene countenances and ethereal presence, glided gracefully towards the assembly. Their mere presence exuded an aura of tranquility and compassion, as if they held the secrets of the universe within their very souls. Alongside them, sages of every sentient form imaginable made their way towards the gathering. From the humble desert-dwelling creatures, who had weathered the harshest of conditions, to the majestic Nagas, with their serpentine bodies and ancient wisdom, the diversity of life was on full display.

But it was not just the earthly beings who graced the assembly. Strange and otherworldly extraterrestrial Bodhisattvas, with their peculiar shapes and sizes, joined the congregation. Their presence was a testament to the vastness of the cosmos, a reminder that enlightenment transcended the boundaries of our own world. And amidst this eclectic gathering, there were also exotic humanoid forms, representing the pinnacle of evolution and the potential for greatness that lay within each individual.

As the last of the attendees took their place, a profound silence settled over the assembly. It was a silence that spoke volumes, a silence pregnant with anticipation and reverence. All eyes were fixed upon the central stage. Tonight was a momentous occasion, the culmination of years of dedication and loyalty. It was the night they would initiate a new member into their esteemed ranks, a night that would forever change the life of one individual.

Evan had spent countless nights studying the ancient texts, deciphering cryptic symbols, and honing his skills in preparation for this very moment. The thought of being chosen as the recipient of the Black Dragon, the highest honor within their clandestine Order, filled him with a mixture of excitement and trepidation.

As the murmurs of conversation gradually subsided, the leader of the Order stepped forward, his presence commanding the attention of all. His voice, deep and resonant, echoed through the chamber as he addressed the gathered members. He spoke of the Order's rich history, its noble purpose, and the significance of the Black Dragon. Each word seemed to hang in the air, heavy with meaning, as the anticipation grew.

And then, with a dramatic pause, the leader announced the name of the chosen one. Evan's heart skipped a beat, his breath caught in his throat. Could it be? Was he truly the one they had deemed worthy of this prestigious honor? The room fell into a hushed silence as all eyes turned towards him, their gazes filled with a mixture of curiosity and admiration.

Evan stepped forward, his legs feeling weak beneath him, but his determination unwavering. He met the leader's gaze, his eyes shining with a newfound sense of purpose. This was his moment, the culmination of years of hard work and dedication. As he approached the center of the chamber, he could feel the weight of the Order's expectations resting upon his shoulders.

The initiation ceremony began, a carefully choreographed dance of ancient rituals and symbolic gestures. Evan followed each step with precision, his mind focused and his heart aflame with a newfound sense of belonging. The whispers of incantations filled the air, their words resonating deep within his soul. He felt a surge of energy coursing through his veins, as if the very essence of the Black Dragon was being infused into his being.

Evan stood before the Grand Black Dragon Supreme, feeling a mix of excitement and nervousness. He had been waiting for this moment for years, and now it was finally happening. The Grand Black Dragon Supreme was a figure of great power and wisdom, and Evan knew that he was about to receive a great honor.
The Grand Black Dragon Supreme, a majestic and imposing figure, motioned for Evan to kneel before him. Evan complied, feeling the cool stone floor beneath his knees as he lowered himself down. The Grand Black Dragon Supreme placed his hands on Evan's head, and began to chant in a beautiful and mesmerizing voice.

As the words flowed from his lips, Evan felt a sense of awe and wonder wash over him. He chanted of the incomparable wisdom of the Black Dragon, and how it had command of Perpetual Vigilance in the Recollective Resolve. He chanted of the inconceivable Buddha-gnosis that the Black Dragon possessed, and how it practiced Tathāgatadhyāna.

The Celebrant continued to chant in melodious verse of how the Black Dragon was baptized with the mark of imagelessness, and had entered into the unsurpassed diamond absorption (vajrasamadhi). He chanted of how the Black Dragon radiated the Mind of one-pointed Contemplation, and abided in the Perfection of Noble Wisdom.

As his voice rose and fell, Evan listened in rapt attention. He heard how the Black Dragon enjoyed the fruits of prajnaparamita, and had abandoned the long night of the carnal mind. He heard how the Black Dragon was devoid of phenomenal outflows, and drank the tea of Absolute Thusness.

The chanting continued, describing of how the Black Dragon donned the robe of the Tathagatas, and sat on the Bodhimaṇḍa (original seat) of the Unborn Mind. He chanted of how the Black Dragon cultivated the Bodhimind and venerates the Mani-pearl, and drank from the cup of irreversibility.

As the Celebrant's voice reached a crescendo, Evan felt a surge of energy course through him. He heard how the Black Dragon generated Mahabodicitta thus perpetuating the Buddhadharma, and turned the light around to protect the Bodhichild. He heard how the Black Dragon shielded the Storehouse of the Tathagatas (Tathagatabgarbha), and slept on the bed of deathlessness.

Finally, the Celebrant chanted of how the Black Dragon was One with Dharmakaya Buddha, and Evan felt a sense of profound peace and understanding wash over him. As the chanting came to an end, Evan remained kneeling before the Grand Black Dragon Supreme, feeling transformed and enlightened by the experience.

And now, the time had come for Evan to experience this extraordinary metamorphosis. His heart raced with a mixture of excitement and trepidation as he was led towards a magnificent jeweled lotus flower throne. The throne seemed to radiate an ethereal glow, as if it held within it the very essence of enlightenment.

Surrounding him were his fellow Bodhisattvas, their presence a testament to their shared journey towards spiritual awakening.

Each Bodhisattva was adorned with necklaces of precious jewels, their brilliance rivaling that of the sun, the moon, or the golden champaka flowers that bloomed in the gardens of paradise. Their eyes sparkled with wisdom and compassion, their serene expressions reflecting the profound peace they had attained.

As Evan settled onto the lotus flower throne, he felt a surge of energy coursing through his veins. It was as if the very fabric of the universe had aligned to witness this sacred event.

And in that moment, as if a mystical energy had beckoned them forth, the majestic Buddhas and Bodhisattvas of the ten directions materialized before their magnificent thrones within the sacred lotus flower palace. The air seemed to shimmer with an ethereal glow as their divine presence graced the hall, illuminating it with a radiant light that seemed to transcend the mortal realm.

Evan, standing in awe, could hardly believe his eyes. The sheer magnificence of these celestial beings left him breathless, their ethereal forms exuding an aura of unparalleled power and wisdom. It was as if the very essence of enlightenment had descended upon this sacred space, filling the air with an indescribable sense of reverence and humility.

Approaching him with a grace that defied earthly limitations, the Buddhas and Bodhisattvas extended their hands, adorned with delicate fragrant oils. The scent wafted through the air, carrying with it a sense of purity and serenity that enveloped Evan's senses. It was as if these divine beings sought to anoint him with their blessings, to bestow upon him a glimpse of their boundless compassion and enlightenment.

Overwhelmed by the weight of their presence, Evan felt a profound sense of gratitude and humility wash over him. In the presence of these enlightened beings, he could not help but feel the insignificance of his own existence, his mortal worries and desires fading into insignificance. It was as if he stood before the very embodiment of wisdom and compassion, and in their presence, he was reminded of the vastness of the universe and the interconnectedness of all beings.

As the Buddhas and Bodhisattvas gently anointed him with their fragrant oils, Evan felt a deep sense of peace and tranquility settle within his being. It was as if their touch carried with it a profound healing energy, soothing his troubled mind and filling his heart with a renewed sense of purpose. In that sacred moment, he understood that he had been granted a rare opportunity, a glimpse into the realm of the divine, and he vowed to carry the wisdom and compassion he had experienced into the world, spreading their light to all who crossed his path.

And so, in the presence of these great Buddhas and Bodhisattvas, Evan stood, forever changed. Their radiance and grace had touched his soul, leaving an indelible mark upon his being. From that day forward, he would walk the path of enlightenment, guided by the wisdom and compassion of these celestial beings.

As the anointing ceremony approached its climax, Evan sensed a profound shift within himself.

Evan's attention was momentarily diverted from the grand ceremony unfolding before him as he caught sight of Pamela, seated among the gathering. His heart swelled with pride and happiness as he saw tears streaming down her cheeks, a clear reflection of the overwhelming joy she felt in witnessing his esteemed initiation.

The room was filled with an air of anticipation and excitement, as Evan and the assembly made their way forward. But amidst the sea of faces, Pamela's eyes widened in astonishment as she noticed Agnes, her dear friend, joining the procession. It was an unexpected surprise that left her speechless.

Agnes, with her graceful presence and radiant smile, had always been a pillar of support for Pamela. She had been there through thick and thin, offering words of encouragement and lending a helping hand whenever needed. Seeing her now, walking alongside Evan, was a testament to the strong bond they all shared.

Pamela couldn't help but feel a surge of emotions welling up within her. It was a bittersweet moment, filled with pride for Evan's achievements and gratitude for Agnes' unwavering friendship. As the procession moved forward, Pamela couldn't turn her eyes away from the two figures, their silhouettes blending seamlessly into the grandeur of the occasion.

In that moment, Pamela realized the true power of friendship and the impact it had on their lives. It was a reminder that they were not alone in their journey, that they had each other to lean on and celebrate their successes together. The sight of Agnes joining Evan on this momentous day only strengthened their bond, reinforcing the unbreakable connection they shared.

As the procession moved further away, Pamela's gaze lingered on Agnes, her dear friend who had become an integral part of their lives. She couldn't help but feel a renewed sense of gratitude for the friendships that had shaped their journey, and the unwavering support that had carried them through every obstacle.

In that moment, as Evan and Agnes disappeared from sight, Pamela made a silent vow to cherish and nurture the bonds they had formed. She knew that their friendship was a rare gem, one that deserved to be treasured and celebrated.

The Reunion

After the grand ceremony of initiation, Pamela found herself in one of the exquisite ante-rooms of the temple. The air was filled with a sense of serenity and anticipation, as if the very walls were whispering ancient secrets. It was in this hallowed space that she unexpectedly crossed paths with Agnes; the sight of Agnes filled Pamela's heart with immense joy, for she had always admired her wisdom and grace.

Unable to contain her excitement, Pamela eagerly approached Agnes and expressed her delight at discovering her once again. She couldn't help but wonder how Agnes had come to be counted among the esteemed Buddhist Black Dragons. It was a title that held great reverence and mystique, and Pamela was curious to know the path that had led Agnes to such an esteemed position.

To Pamela's surprise, Agnes gently corrected her, explaining that the designation of Black Dragons was not determined by sectarian means, but rather by a universal association with supernal truths. It was not a title bestowed upon individuals based on their religious affiliations, but rather a recognition of their profound connection to the divine.

With a serene smile, Agnes went on to enlighten Pamela about the illustrious figures who had been considered Black Dragons throughout history. She mentioned the names of Meister Eckhart, Teresa of Avila and John of the Cross, three renowned mystics whose wisdom and spiritual insights were deemed inconceivable. These luminaries had been granted the privilege of being counted among the Black Dragons due to their profound understanding of the mystical realm.

Agnes humbly revealed that she, too, had been bestowed with this honor, thanks to her own mystical Unborn and Unknowing association. It was a privilege she held close to her heart, a testament to her unwavering dedication to the pursuit of divine truths. As Pamela listened to Agnes speak, she couldn't help but feel a deep sense of awe and admiration for her dear friend.

In that sacred moment, surrounded by the ethereal beauty of the temple, Pamela realized that the path to enlightenment was not confined to any particular religious doctrine. It was a journey that transcended boundaries and embraced seekers from all walks of life. And as she stood there, basking in the presence of Agnes, she understood that true wisdom and spiritual enlightenment were not limited to any one tradition, but rather a universal quest for truth and understanding.

Agnes, with a warm smile on her face, expressed her own overwhelming joy at the unexpected reunion with her dear friend, Pamela. It had been quite some time since they last crossed paths, and Agnes couldn't help but feel a sense of pride as she had been silently observing Pamela's progress along the Unborn spiritual path.

As they settled into a quiet corner, Agnes leaned in closer, her voice filled with a mix of excitement and anticipation. She knew that Pamela possessed something truly extraordinary, a gift that set her apart from the rest. It was a gift that couldn't be seen with the naked eye, but its impact was undeniable to those fortunate enough to receive it in its ephemeral form.

"My dearest Pamela," Agnes began, her voice filled with genuine affection, "you are truly blessed to exist in this world, for you possess something truly remarkable. It is a gift that transcends the physical realm, something intangible yet profoundly tangible to those who are open to receiving it."

Agnes paused for a moment, allowing her words to sink in. She could see the curiosity and intrigue in Pamela's eyes, eager to uncover the depths of her own potential. Agnes continued, her voice now laced with a sense of urgency.

"However, my dear, there is still much work to be done. The path you have embarked upon is not an easy one. It requires dedication, perseverance, and a willingness to delve deep into the recesses of your soul. The Unborn spiritual path is a journey of self-discovery, a quest to unlock the hidden treasures within yourself and share them with the world."

Pamela listened intently, her heart swelling with a mixture of excitement and trepidation. She had always felt a calling, a sense that there was something greater she was meant to contribute to the world. And now, with Agnes by her side, guiding her along this mystical path, she felt a renewed sense of purpose.

Agnes reached out and gently clasped Pamela's hands, her touch radiating warmth and reassurance. "Fear not, my dear Pamela, for you are not alone on this journey. I will be here every step of the way, guiding you, supporting you, and helping you navigate the challenges that lie ahead. Together, we will uncover the depths of your potential and illuminate the lives of those who are fortunate enough to cross your path."

Pamela felt a surge of gratitude wash over her; she knew that she had been given a rare opportunity to showcase her exceptional talents and abilities on the mystical path of the Unborn. It was a privilege that she cherished deeply, and one that she was determined to make the most of. She had always felt a deep connection to the Unborn, and had spent countless hours studying its teachings and exploring its mysteries. Now, she was being given the chance to put her knowledge and skills to the test, and to share her insights with others who were also on the path.

She knew that the road ahead would be long and challenging, but she was ready for whatever lay ahead. She had spent years preparing for this moment, honing her skills and perfecting her craft. Now, it was time to put all of that hard work to the test.

She knew that her journey was far from over, but she was ready for whatever lay ahead. With her talents and abilities, and her deep connection to the Unborn, she knew that she could accomplish anything she set her mind to.

As Pamela's gaze wandered across Agnes' attire, her eyes were suddenly captivated by the glimmering silver medallion hanging around Agnes' neck. It was a beautiful piece, adorned with an intricate image of the Great Other Tree. However, something caught Pamela's attention - a new branch had sprung on the image, intertwining with the existing ones.

Curiosity piqued, Pamela couldn't help but inquire about the unexpected addition. Agnes, with a warm smile on her face, explained that the emergence of the extra branch was a direct result of Pamela's own personal growth. She attributed it to the profound connection they shared, suggesting that her association with Pamela had sparked a transformative journey within her.

Pamela's heart swelled with a mixture of surprise and delight. She had always admired Agnes' wisdom and grace, but to think that her own presence had played a role in Agnes' growth was truly humbling. It was a testament to the power of their bond and the profound impact they had on each other's lives.

As they continued their conversation, Pamela couldn't help but reflect on the significance of the silver medallion and the Great Other Tree. It symbolized not only their shared journey but also the interconnectedness of all living beings. Just as the branches of the tree intertwined and grew together, so did their lives, forever entwined in a beautiful tapestry of growth and transformation.

From that moment on, Pamela cherished the medallion as a tangible reminder of the profound connection she shared with Agnes. It served as a constant source of inspiration, reminding her of the power of friendship and the transformative potential that lies within each and every one of us.

A Farewell

Agnes turned to me with a solemn expression on her face. She informed me that Evan would be speaking with me presently and asked me to brace myself for what he had to say. My heart sank as I realized that this was going to be a difficult conversation. Agnes explained that Evan had to take leave of me now and remain for an unforeseeable time in the Temple of the Black Dragons.

I felt a lump form in my throat as I tried to process the news. Evan was one of my closest friends and the thought of him leaving was almost unbearable. Agnes must have sensed my distress because she placed a comforting hand on my shoulder and offered me a sympathetic smile. Pamela was deeply distraught, but managed to put a smile on her face as Evan approached.

Evan stood tall and confident, his figure adorned in the majestic Black Dragon robes. The intricate patterns and rich black fabric seemed to amplify his presence, exuding an air of resilience and strength. As he glanced around, his eyes met Agnes', and he knew he had to ask her to leave them alone for a while. There was something he needed to share, something deeply personal that he wished to convey to Pamela privately.

With a gentle yet firm voice, Evan addressed Agnes, kindly requesting her departure. He understood the importance of privacy in this moment, knowing that what he was about to reveal required a certain level of intimacy. Agnes, though slightly taken aback, respected his wishes and gracefully excused herself from their presence.

As Agnes left, the room seemed to hold its breath, anticipation hanging in the air. Evan took a deep breath, his eyes scanning Pamela's face, searching for understanding and support. Pamela, his closest companion, was eager to hear what he had to say, sensing the weight of his words even before they were spoken.

"With a heavy heart and a sense of duty weighing upon my shoulders, I find myself compelled to bid you farewell, Pamela. The time has come for me to embark on a new chapter of my life, one that requires my undivided attention and unwavering commitment. As I stand before you, my voice trembling with a mixture of excitement and trepidation, I must confess that my newfound responsibilities within the hallowed walls of the Temple of the Black Dragons beckon me forth.

"Oh, how I wish I could linger a while longer in your comforting presence, relishing in the warmth of our conversations and the shared laughter that has become the very essence of our friendship. Alas, destiny has cast its die, and I must heed its call. The Temple, with its ancient secrets and enigmatic rituals, has chosen me as its guardian, its servant, and I dare not deny its request.

"In the depths of my being, I feel a profound sense of awe and reverence for the Temple's sacred halls, where the whispers of forgotten wisdom echo through time. It is within those hallowed chambers that I shall immerse myself in the teachings of the Black Dragons, an order steeped in mysticism and revered for their unparalleled mastery of the arcane arts. The weight of this honor, this privilege, is not lost upon me, for I am but a humble soul, chosen to walk the path of enlightenment.

"As I prepare to embark on this extraordinary journey, I cannot help but reflect upon the countless memories we have woven together, like a tapestry of shared experiences and cherished moments. From the first day we met, our lives intertwined in a dance of camaraderie and mutual understanding. We have laughed, we have cried, and we have weathered the storms of life side by side. Your unwavering support and unwavering belief in me have been the pillars upon which I have built my courage, my determination.

"Yet, as I stand here, on the precipice of a new beginning, I implore you to understand the gravity of my decision. The Temple of the Black Dragons beckons me with its mystical song, promising a path of enlightenment and self-discovery that I cannot ignore. It is a calling that resonates deep within my soul, urging me to embrace the unknown, to delve further into the mysteries that lie beyond the veil of ordinary existence."

Pamela's voice trembled with a mix of understanding and sorrow as she spoke, her words carefully chosen to convey the depth of her emotions. "I can understand your position," she began, her voice soft yet resolute, "but the weight of your absence in my life will be felt with a profound intensity. It is as if a part of myself, a cherished fragment of who I am, is now slipping away, never to be experienced again."

Her eyes, once filled with warmth and affection, now glistened with unshed tears, reflecting the pain that resided within her heart. The bond they had shared, the connection that had woven their lives together, was now unraveling before her very eyes. It was a bittersweet realization, for she understood the reasons behind their parting, yet the ache of losing someone so dear was undeniable.

Pamela's mind wandered back to the countless memories they had created together, the laughter and tears and spiritual insight they had shared, and the dreams they had nurtured side by side. Each moment, once vibrant and alive, now seemed to fade into the recesses of her mind, like a distant echo that would soon be forgotten. The thought of never experiencing those precious moments again was a heavy burden to bear.

She had always believed that their connection was unbreakable, an unspoken promise that they would weather any storm together. But now, as the reality of their separation settled upon her, she couldn't help but feel a profound sense of loss. It was as if a vital piece of her existence was being stripped away, leaving behind an emptiness that seemed impossible to fill.

Pamela's heart ached with the knowledge that their paths were diverging, leading them towards separate destinies. She knew that life was a journey of constant change, and sometimes, even the most cherished relationships had to evolve or dissolve. But accepting this truth did little to ease the pain that now consumed her.

Evan stood tall and confident, his eyes fixed on his companion. "You must not lose heart," he said, his voice steady and reassuring. "Though we for now turn our separate ways, I'm confident that down that mystic road of the Unborn our paths will one day cross again."

Pamela looked at him with a mixture of sadness and hope. They had been through so much together, and now it was time to part ways. But Evan's words gave her comfort, a glimmer of hope that they would meet again.

As they stood there in one of the majestic hallways of the Temple, Evan continued to speak. "Our journey has been long and difficult, but we have learned so much. We have faced our fears and overcome them, we have fought against the darkness and emerged victorious. And now, as we go our separate ways, we carry with us the knowledge and strength we have gained."

Pamela nodded, her eyes shining with gratitude. Evan had been a true friend and mentor, guiding her through the trials and tribulations of their journey. And now, as they said their goodbyes, she knew that she would always carry Evan's words with her, a beacon of hope in the darkness.

But before they departed, Evan placed an object into Pamela's hands. It was the mystical dagger, the legendary Phurba, renowned for its power and the tales of its triumph over the infamous Aleister Crowley. Evan believed that Pamela would have need of it one day, and he wanted her to be prepared. The weight of the dagger felt heavy in her palms, as if it carried the weight of countless battles fought and won.

Looking into Pamela's eyes, Evan spoke softly, his voice filled with a mixture of concern and determination. He urged her to remember the Phurba's mantra, for it held the key to awakening the inner deity within it. Chanting those sacred words would summon forth a force so pure and divine that it would banish all evil in its wake. He also taught her how to roll the Phurba in her hands as she chanted the deity's sacred mantra.

Pamela listened intently, her heart pounding with a mixture of fear and excitement. She understood the significance of Evan's gift and the responsibility it carried. The Phurba was not just a weapon, but a symbol of their shared journey and the trust Evan had placed in her.

As she held the dagger close to her chest, Pamela vowed to honor Evan's trust and protect their cause. She would carry the Phurba with her always, ready to unleash its power when the time came. And she would never forget the mantra, for it held the key to unlocking her inner strength and vanquishing any darkness that dared to cross her path.

With a final embrace, Evan and Pamela bid each other farewell, their hearts heavy with the weight of their impending separation. But they knew that their destinies were intertwined, and that their paths would cross again. And when that day came, Pamela would be armed with the Phurba, ready to face whatever challenges lay ahead, guided by the mantra that would also awaken the divine within her.

End of Book One

Made in the USA
Middletown, DE
20 November 2023